A Land of Ash

an Anthology by David Dalglish

Table of Contents:

A Land of Ash

One Last Dinner Party
by David Dalglish

"Try and hurry back," Wilma told Oren as he climbed into his rusted blue Ford. "If you're out too long I'll get worried, and it's a devil to put blush on when my face gets red like it does."

"Don't you worry," said her husband. "Ring the Pankratz while I'm gone. Maybe they'll change their minds."

"I don't think they will," she said. "They have family down in Texas, though god knows what the roads look like since the…"

"Just try."

He drove into town, dirt billowing behind his truck. The Dollar Store would have been cheaper, but he turned down Main instead for Hank's Groceries. Hank waited outside, his ankles crossed, his arms calmly folded over his belly, and a loaded shotgun tilted upward by his feet. Oren pulled up, shoved it into park, and shut off the ignition.

"Morning," Hank shouted as the roaring engine died. "I was wondering if you'd show."

"Yeah," Oren said. While climbing out, he made a grunting noise and gestured to the shotgun. "Hope you haven't had to use that."

"I've let people take what they want," Hank said. His voice sounded tired, and the puffy darkness below his eyes signified tears, drink, or both. "The first couple families cleared me out. The rest wander around like stunned mules. I let 'em see everything's gone, and then they go, usually holding something weird. You know those filters for the big window air conditioners? Had a guy walk out holding ten, all I had. What in Jesus's name he think he's going to do with them?"

"I'm sorry," Oren said, as if the whole mess were his fault. He certainly sounded like he thought it was his fault.

"Think nothing of it," Hank said. "Though I'm glad to be talking to someone who's not waving a gun in my face. You hear about the Dollar Store?"

Oren turned to the side, spat, and then shook his head.

"Glenda lock it up tight, I take it?" he asked.

"Not like it did any good. There's a reason my door is wide open, Oren, because if it weren't, I doubt you and Wilma would ever see my ugly face again. Besides, not like money means anything, not anymore."

Oren glanced inside. Every wall and shelf was stripped bare. He caught a puddle of what looked like milk spilled across the floor of one aisle, apple sauce in another. He felt a bit of pity for old Hank, and he clapped the guy once on the shoulder.

"Looks like me and Wilma will make do with what we have at the house," he said. "You're welcome to come with."

"Nah," Hank said. He glanced back at his store, and he looked uncomfortable and embarrassed. "I planned on climbing up to the roof, drag up one of my lawn chairs, and sit up there. And wait, you know? When did they say the whole shitstorm would start?"

"About four-thirty," Oren said. "Though you never know. Weathermen are hardly better than the farmer's almanac. Hell, a coin flip does better than them, I heard once."

"Yeah?" said Hank. "I think they're right about this one, though. They wouldn't dare fuck this up. I take it your radio's out, too?"

"Every station. I checked on the drive here."

A bit of awkward silence followed, and at last Oren turned to his truck. When he waved, a bit of the hardness in Hank's face broke.

"You know," Hank said. "I stashed a few things when I heard. Not much, not like the hoarders with their water and flour and god knows what else. But enough for a good meal. I'll come by in a bit, once I say goodbye to the old place. Thirty years. Thirty goddamn years, mopping the floor with my sweat and paying bills with my blood. And for what, Oren? For what?"

He looked ready to cry. Oren frowned, not accustomed to such easy emotions from another man. Unsure of what to do, he hopped into his truck and slammed the door.

"Come say hello to Wilma," he said. "She'd like that."

"She's a sweet gal," said Hank. "Anyone else going to be there?"

Oren started the truck. As the engine banged, he continued talking, the satisfying rumble easing the nerves he had felt building during his conversation.

"Wilma's trying the Pankratz," he half-shouted. "Don't think they'll be coming. The Williams will be there. Kids were living in California, so Thelma's pretty shook up, and Roy isn't taking it much better. They needed the company, so…"

His voice trailed off. Hank resumed leaning against the front of his store and braced the shotgun across his lap.

"Go straight home," he shouted. "Stay away from the highway; the roads are hell right now."

Oren had a thought to tell him that the whole world would soon be hell, not just the highway, but kept his mouth shut. He drove home to his wife.

Wilma had done well applying her blush, along with the rest of her makeup. She had on a modest white dress and her finest jewelry. Oren felt a tug of memory at the

forty Easter services he had attended with his wife. They'd
had two kids, and through fevers, snot, tantrums, and
teenage rebellion, they'd dragged them into their small
community church year after year. Their eldest, Julie, had
married a German man at college and moved to New York.
They'd managed to talk with her about two minutes before
the cell phones went dead. Julie had sounded scared but
holding together well.

"I wish I was home, daddy," she said only moments
before the static. "That's all I want right now, I want to
be…"

Oren wiped a tear from his cheek. A part of him was
glad that his son Jerry was not alive to see everyone so
afraid. He'd been born slow in the head. He could wipe his
ass, but that was the most complex set of actions he could
manage by himself. A seizure had claimed him in his
thirties. He might have lived, Oren had told the lawyers
that, but the home had been too full of difficult patients
and poorly-trained attendees. His son had died thrashing
and shitting himself, unable to call for help, and by the time
someone noticed, he'd nearly chewed off his own tongue.

Poor Jerry, he thought. *Never could watch nothing but Disney
shows. Hospitals are crowded so bad they're worthless; that's what the
television said before it went blank, anyway. God, what would it be
like at a rest home? Would the nurses even stay?*

He doubted it. He felt pity for all the elderly and
retarded, but he clamped that emotion down. Pity was a
dangerous thing, for there were too many, just too many,
and a man could become overwhelmed. There were the
elderly, the sick, the pregnant, the nursing, the little babes,
the orphans, the poor…they'd die. All of them. Just like
the rest of North America.

Hell, if he was going to pity anyone, he'd pity Wilma
and himself.

"Did they have any?" Wilma asked as Oren got out of his truck.

He shook his head.

"Cleaned out. He didn't have a lick of spit left to sell."

The wrinkles on his wife's face pulled back tight across her jaw.

"Not even the zucchini? Cripes, no one liked it before, but I can't make my lasagna without it, Oren. I thought, surely, it's just zucchini, they'll take the water and the flour and the meat, but not the zucchini…"

She wasn't crying; she more appeared to be leaking out the corners of her eyes. Her voice never wavered. Oren wrapped his arms around her and held her tight. He felt her quivering against his chest, and he had a strange image of himself as a child holding a scared rabbit.

"You'll make do," he said. "We raised two kids on water and hope. You can manage your lasagna without zucchini."

Wilma sniffed. When she pulled back, she reminded him less of a rabbit and more like an old tree, its bark peeling and its leaves fallen, but the roots still firm in the ground. He kissed her cheek, and she smiled at him.

"You're right," she said. "Not often, but when you are, you are."

Oren was not much for baking, and even with the end of the world approaching, he felt awkward in the kitchen. After a few clumsy attempts at separating pasta and chopping tomatoes, his little bat of a wife ushered him out the door.

"Go get a fire going," she said. "Thelma will be fine with my lasagna, but you know Roy. If it wasn't mooing, he don't want it."

Three squirts of lighter fluid were enough to get the charcoal going. He'd known others that'd drown the coals with fluid for an easy light, but that felt wasteful to Oren. It seemed a silly thing to worry about, but some habits are hard to break after sixty-five years, and that was one.

They'd kept a giant freezer full of meat on their porch ever since they bought their first pig thirty years ago. A few of their neighbors had swung by since morning, right after the news first hit the air. They all had a desperate, embarrassed look on their faces, as if they were ashamed to steal but knowing they would anyway. Sighing, Oren gently nudged the coals about with a poker, trying to forget that he was building his last fire.

What the hell, he thought. He grabbed the lighter fluid and gave it a healthy squeeze. With a satisfying roar, it flared high above the grill. Oren jumped backward, letting out a 'whoa' before laughing. It felt good to laugh.

The first of the steaks was on the grill when Thelma and Roy pulled up in a brown Chevy that was ten years passed its date with a junkyard. Oren continued plopping down and flipping steaks, preferring to let his wife handle the initial greeting. From the corner of his eye, he saw them climb out of the car. Thelma wore a black dress and an old hat that reminded him of Jackie Kennedy. Roy, meanwhile, wore a tux that had served him reliably for the past ten years.

Absurd, thought Oren as his wife wrapped them both in a hug. *My wife's going to Easter, Roy a wedding, and Thelma a funeral. What's so wrong with jeans? If I'm going to die, I'll die comfortable, not like a stuffed Barbie doll.*

His wife led Thelma into the den while Roy wandered over to check on the fire. It was a habit of his; quite possibly a habit of every man. All roaring fires needed communal assessment.

"Looking good," Roy said, sounding as if Oren should be pleased by his seal of approval. "Hotter than normal for you, though. In a hurry?"

"We've got an hour," Oren said. "And I'll be damned if I don't get to eat my steak first."

He stole a glance at Roy. The man had a haggard look to his face, and his bloodshot eyes made him look damned, steak or not.

"Thelma baked up a pie," Roy said. "Well, cobbler really. Peach. It was Randy's favorite, you know? His…" His words drifted off, and Oren kept his eyes fixed on the fire so he didn't have to see the tears.

"We had no word from there," Roy said after composing himself. "News said the satellites and radios were knocked out immediately. But the winds coming from the ocean, they might push it away, right? Randy and Susan are south of Yellowstone, maybe it's far enough, and the winds will just push it our way. You think there's a chance of that, Oren? Do you?"

Oren flipped a steak.

"No," he said. He could imagine the tiny thread of hope that his friend clung to, and while a part of him thought to let him hang on, another couldn't bear to lie. "I don't think so, Roy. Not from what I was hearing. Not from what the TV was showing."

Roy nodded. More tears ran down his cheeks, but he wasn't sobbing, and his voice was firm when he talked.

"I can keep hoping though, right? Who knows, I may walk up to Jesus and ask for my little boy and girl, and he'll look at me like I'm a simple-minded fool and say, 'You beat them here, Roy, but don't you worry, time flies up here, it'll fly, and before you know you'll be seeing them again.' You don't know everything, Oren, and that damn TV knows even less."

"I reckon you're right," Oren said, though he didn't think he was.

Hank arrived when they were pulling the steaks off the grill. The two women had joined them outside, iced drinks in hand. When Hank stepped out of his Ford, he held a giant 24-pack of Bud like it was a basket of gold.

"Nothing I had could match your cooking," Hank said to Wilma. "But this here's something."

Wilma accepted a can, but Thelma refused. Her makeup had run from a recent crying fit. Her wig was askew, revealing a bit of the gray underneath. She looked much like a deer staring at a pair of oncoming headlights, baffled and unable to move. They were all like that, Oren realized. Soon they'd see headlights in the western sky, and they'd stare in wonder. Like the deer, they'd stayed put, unmoving, unblinking, waiting for its approach.

Oren hoped it'd be quick, like a speeding car, and hurt for even less.

The steaks finished before the lasagna. Oren slapped a few hot dogs on the fire, doubting anyone would eat them but seeing no point in keeping them. As they cooked, he listened as Thelma told stories about their children to Wilma while Roy quietly sipped a beer nearby. The tales of diaper changes and midnight scares and faulty pregnancy tests brought Oren's mind back to Julie in New York, and he wished that Thelma would talk about something else. Their life was soon to end; did they have to sulk about it?

Shame they cancelled the baseball games, he thought. *Could use a good distraction.*

The two women went inside, and after a moment, Roy followed.

"He looks like hell," Hank said, crunching up an empty can in his fist.

"We all do," Oren said.

Hank chuckled, still holding the can. A queer smile crossed his face, and looking like a naughty schoolchild, he tossed it to the ground.

"Might make an Indian cry," he said, "but I think they got bigger things to shed tears for lately."

"I'll drink to that," Oren said. "God, I just want to watch one more ball game. Cardinals had a shot this year, you know? Seems silly, but I always knew I'd go one day, and Wilma probably soon after, but the Cardinals...they're supposed to go on forever. No more seasons, now. No more records. No more playoffs. It's a goddamn shame."

Oren piled the hot dogs onto a large plate, directly atop the steaks. When he glanced up, he saw Wilma at the door wearing a look he knew well.

"Supper's ready," he told Hank. "Let's get to it."

They ate outside. The weather had already grown chillier, but none of them could bear the idea of being cooped up indoors. They piled their plates atop a circular white patio table, devouring lasagna and steaks and beer with ravenous appetites. Even Wilma, a notorious light eater, devoured two helpings of lasagna plus a third of a dog.

Conversation remained light until Thelma said what had obviously been on her mind the whole day.

"Today's the Rapture," she announced. "It has to be. God wouldn't let our good Christian nation be wiped out unless he's preparing for the end."

"I don't know," Hank said. "The local stations lasted a bit longer than the cable, and they had on a little spitfire in a suit shouting about how this was our punishment. We've gotten too sinful, you know? We're like a modern day Sodom, and hallelujah, we're all about to become pillars of salt."

He chuckled, but Oren saw no humor in it. He didn't think either of them was right, but he sure wasn't going to say so. Thelma flushed a deep red, as if insulted that someone might disagree.

"If the Rapture's come," Hank continued, "then why are you still here?"

Shut your mouth, Oren thought. *Just shut your damn mouth.*

"Because," Thelma said, "the angels are in the clouds. They'll get us when it hits, just like they got Randy and Susan."

"There ain't no angels in that fucking cloud!" Hank was shouting but didn't appear to know it. "If Randy and Susan are in heaven, they got there the old fashioned way; by coughing until their lungs bled and their eyeballs…"

"Enough!" Oren shouted. His abrupt stand knocked his little plastic chair sprawling. He glared at Hank, who stared back with tears in his eyes.

"You got ten minutes," Oren said. "Maybe you should go back to your store. You can take my chair."

"I reckon I'd rather stay," Hank said. He glanced over to Thelma. "I'm sorry, really I am. Just scared is all. I hope you're right. Never considered myself a good Christian man, but I think today I'm terrified enough to try. Think the angels will grab me?"

Thelma was too busy wiping at her tears, but Wilma piped in with her usual perfect timing.

"Bible says god refuses no man who asks humbly enough," she said. "Humble ain't your nature, Hank. Try it for today, and we might all make it through just fine. Right, Oren?"

"Right," he said.

Everyone pushed away their food. Wilma brought out the peach cobbler and spooned out massive servings for everyone. Oren could only pick at it. Cobbler might have been Randy's favorite, but it sure wasn't his. When he looked around, he noticed no one else was eating, either. It was his fault, he realized.

Ten minutes, I shouted. What is wrong with me? Why'd I have to remind everyone?

But now it was only eight minutes. Oren felt almost angry at the clock. It had crawled by all day, but once he was with friends, it burst into a frantic sprint. All around were sad smiles and faces wet with tears. What a way to end the world: together at one last dinner party, sobbing like children and snarling at each other like dogs.

"Let's get the chairs over to the front lawn," Oren said. "We're all thinking it, so let's stop pretending. We'll get a good look at the western sky from there."

"Are you sure?" Wilma asked. "We've still got some time before…"

"I'm sure," Oren said, and that ended the discussion.

Wilma and Oren sat next to each other on their lawn chairs. Hank sat opposite them and the Williams. Oren thanked god for small favors. Once positioned, they took their beers (even Thelma had one) and toasted the sky. The clouds were soft and gray, but looming behind them seemed to be a storm thick with a substance more solid than rain and more frightening than thunder. Oren checked his watch. Five minutes at the most, assuming the weathermen knew what they were doing.

"Breathe in deep," Hank said to no one in particular. "I heard that makes it quickest. Coughing only drags it out."

The left side of Thelma's face twitched, but she held her tongue.

A breeze picked up from the west, so sudden in its strength that Thelma had no time to grab her hat before it sailed across the lawn. For a moment, she looked ready to chase after, and then decided otherwise. The clouds rolled across the sky, pushed on by an unseen wave. Another gust of wind hit them, and it was surprisingly warm. Oren felt Wilma grab his hand and squeeze it tight. He squeezed back.

The clouds broke, and the sun shone down on them from a beautiful blue sky. The wind seemed to pause for a moment, as if respectful of the momentary calm. Oren heard a little 'oh' from his wife, and even Hank grunted in surprise. When the wind returned, and clouds shadowed their faces, Oren felt like the last remnant of peace in the world had died.

"Will it hurt?" Thelma asked.

"Just a cough," Hank replied. "Just like a bad cough."

Rolling toward them, an eager minute early, was the ash cloud from the Yellowstone Caldera's eruption. It grumbled dark and thick, and within it they saw lightning. A soft white, like the foam of a wave, rushed ahead. With a blast of hot air, they felt it hit. Like a desert wind, it burned the back of their throats and nostrils. Roy shouted something, but Oren could not hear him. Then the air slowed, although the heat remained. The light of the sun faded. The roar left their ears.

"Look," Oren said, his mouth dropping open in surprise. Falling in thick, twirling pieces was what looked like snow. It fell upon their hands, their hair, their faces. It was warm to the touch. When they brushed it across their skin, it left a gray smear.

"Sweet Jesus," said Wilma.

The rest of the ash cloud covered the sky, ramming away the white. It was so thick, so monstrous, that night fell. Oren felt his wife's hand tremble in his, and he clutched it tight. High above, thunder roared.

In the darkness, Thelma was the first to cough.

Alone on the Mountain
By David McAfee

3 Days Left

He lived off the grid. He hadn't had the opportunity to talk to anyone in years, but if he had, that's what he would have told them; that he lived off the grid. His house was a shallow cave in the side of the mountain. The lip of the cave, along with the slight overhang, kept the rain out, and during the winter his door - nothing more than a few branches woven together and covered in brush to make it like foliage - kept the heat in. He'd chosen the place because of the natural chimney at the back. He could light a fire to keep the cave warm while the smoke traveled through the crack in the ceiling and went only God knew where.

Additionally, the cave's position in the mountainside afforded him an incredible view of the valley below. If a bear or a deer walked by, he'd know about it long before the animal knew he was close.

It worked on people, too.

Granted, few humans came this way. But every once in a while some hiker would get lost or some would-be survivalist tromped through the valley. Even a handful of hunters had come through here over the years, with their bright orange vests and the smell of soap that even he could smell from a hundred feet away. No wonder they never caught anything. They didn't know how to truly blend in. Most of the time they kept on moving, never even looking up.

They miss so much that way, he thought. *Eyes on the ground or on the trees around them, watching for predators. If only they'd look up.*

Still, it suited him. The less time they spent in his world, the less likely they were to find him. Even after fifteen years, he still lived in fear that someday others would find him and bring him back. Not that he had much to go back to. But they'd try. Oh, Hell yes, they would try. He could picture it now.

Don't you miss running water?

A creek ran at the base of the valley. Plenty of running water.

What about your family?

Fuck 'em. They're probably all dead by now, anyway.

But the world has changed so much. There have been so many advances.

Keep 'em. I'm fine right here.

He didn't actually know if there had been any advances; it was just a guess. The fact was there were always advances out there. Everything needed to be better, smarter, faster, or stronger. The world got itself in a big ass hurry and didn't want to slow down to see what it was running from. So fuck 'em. Fuck all of 'em.

Out here the only thing that ever changed was the weather, and he liked it that way. This time of year, the squirrels darted around the valley floor, gathering food for the coming winter. The deer would be storing some extra body fat and growing thicker fur. Soon they'd be surviving on moss and tree bark. Every Fall, it was the same thing.

He looked down into the valley below, prepared to count the squirrels. He'd named a few of them, and spoke their names when they came into view. But he was never really sure if they were the same. All the squirrels looked alike after a few years. Besides, it made it harder to eat them if you named 'em.

For a minute, he couldn't tell what was wrong with the picture, but then it hit him. There were no squirrels. No deer, either. Now that he thought about it, he hadn't seen any all day. Strange. The woods were usually teaming with the little chatterboxes this time of year. Could there be people in his valley? Maybe they scared off all the game. He'd have to check it out. Squirrels weren't the only ones who needed to store food for the winter.

He got to his feet, but stumbled as a feeling of vertigo took him and his knee gave way, making him fall on his ass. The years were catching up to him, it seemed. Soon the pain in his knuckles would be so severe he doubted he'd be able to numb them with herbs anymore. But the alternative was unthinkable. He couldn't go back. Not after so many years out here. He'd just have to deal with—

Strange, the vertigo should have passed when he sat down, but instead it grew even more intense. He stared at the trees in the valley, noting how they, too, seemed to be swaying on unsteady legs. Then he realized the truth.

His legs weren't unsteady, the ground was.

Earthquake, he thought, *and a hum-dinger, too.* There hadn't been a quake in his remote section of eastern Kentucky in years. Not since right after he came here. And none this severe. He looked up and saw that several large rocks had come loose and were bounding down the mountain toward him. He scrambled to his feet and ducked into his cave just as a rock about two feet across slammed the spot where he'd been standing only a moment ago.

Staying in the cave wasn't smart. If the quake got any worse the whole thing could collapse. But stepping out into a rainstorm of rocks and rubble seemed an equally bad idea. He was just trying to figure out on which death he should take his chances when the quake stopped. It didn't ease off or slow down to a steady rumble, it just quit, as suddenly as it began.

He stood at the entrance of the cave, listening to the sound of birds as they returned to the valley. Soon the squirrels were back, too. Bouncing along and picking up nuts and acorns. Chattering and running through the valley in their search for food.

Weird. It almost seemed like the animals had been expecting the quake.

He shook the thought from his mind and grabbed his sling. He had a shotgun, but he'd long ago run out of shells. Over the last decade, he'd gotten damn handy with a strip of cloth and a baseball sized rock, though, and he could take out a deer from thirty steps away. He stepped out of the cave and into the valley, reminding himself that food would be scarce in the coming months.

By the time he returned to his cave with half a dozen dead squirrels and a wild turkey slung over his shoulder, he'd forgotten all about the quake.

2 Days Left

He sat outside on the ledge, drying the meat over hot coals. He'd need a lot of it to get through the winter. Not that he wouldn't be able to hunt at all; the game would still be around, there would just be less of it. Far better to have too much dried meat and not need it all than to run out halfway through the winter because he thought a deer might happen by. He was never a boy scout, but he still liked being prepared. After fifteen years on his mountain, he knew how to make it through the cold winter.

Once the meat was suitably dried out, he stuffed it into a pouch. The pouch was made of deerskin and lined with a wax he made by melting animal fats and combining it with tree sap. Completely watertight. He hung it on the back wall, next to half a dozen others. Seven bags of food in all. Still not quite enough. But if he could bag a deer this afternoon, that should make up the difference. He grabbed his sling and a handful of stones, and after a moment took his old BEAR compound bow from the wall and grabbed his three remaining arrows. He tested the string. The wax-coated nylon had held up well. He thought it would last another season or two before he had to replace it. He might be able to make a suitable string out of deer hide, but he didn't know for sure and hadn't been willing to risk finding out yet.

Satisfied that he was ready, he stepped out into the sunlight.

The valley stretched out below him, a breathtaking sea of reds, yellows, and oranges. Here and there a few still-green leaves held on to their chlorophyll, and of course the pines and firs still bore green needles, but for the most part the valley looked like God had splashed a bucket of paint on it and walked away. The Appalachian Mountain chain was so beautiful this time of year. He stood at the mouth of his cave, taking in the view.

This is why I left Nashville, he thought. *Right here. right now. This could be Heaven.*

Except in Heaven, he probably wouldn't be hungry.

After a few minutes spent admiring the view, he trundled down the side of the mountain, watching for any sign of deer or bear. There were also mountain lions, coyotes, and even a few wolves scattered around the area, so he stayed on full watch. Coyotes would leave him alone unless he looked weak or sick, and wolves would lose him if he took to the trees. But if he met up with a mountain lion...well, he just hoped he didn't run into one. That was the reason for the bow. He wouldn't use the arrows on game, it was too easy to lose or break one. But his sling wouldn't do any good against a hungry cat that outweighed him by eighty pounds.

Once he reached the valley floor, he headed left. About two miles south of his cave was a secluded spring where deer often congregated. It should be easy enough to kill one once he arrived. He didn't usually go that far while hunting, especially when his hands hurt, but a single deer could finish off his stores and make sure he had enough to eat all winter long. For that kind of peace of mind, he'd make the trip.

About halfway to the spring he noticed the woods around him went quiet again. His feet made a slight crinkle as he walked through the dead pine needles and dried out leaves, not even fifteen years could erase all the sounds of his passage, but his steps sounded a little louder without the background noise of the woods to diffuse it.

He stopped to listen. Nothing. Not a single bird, squirrel, or even field mouse made its presence known. Weird. It felt almost like the animals were afraid.

Then he heard it. Animals. Big ones. Somewhere behind him, and not far. Not the high pitched yip of a coyote, but the deeper, stronger bark of wolves. He turned around just in time to see a big one leap through the trees twenty yards away and run right at him. An instant later, two more bounded from the brush.

Shit.

He turned and ran, hoping to get to a sturdy pine about fifty feet away. The low branch would be perfect to haul himself up, if only he could get there. The sounds of the wolves at his back grew louder, their barks and yips coming closer to his heels. By the sound of it, several more wolves had joined the first three. The entire pack must be right behind him, but he didn't want to turn his head and risk tripping over a root or rock.

Twenty five feet to go. The first wolf was only a few feet behind him. He would never make it.

So this is how it ends, he thought.

The first wolf was right on top of him. He could hear the big canine's labored breath. He could almost feel it on the back of his neck. A few more steps and those teeth would be in his calf, or his hamstring, or maybe even the back of his neck. In his last seconds, he whispered a prayer, asking for a quick death. Just a few steps more...

The wolf ran by him without stopping. The other wolves in the pack did likewise.

It took him a moment to realize he wasn't dead yet, but as the fourth wolf passed him by without so much as a glance he reached the pine. Not willing to take a chance on any of the other wolves, he grabbed the branch and hauled himself up. He reached for the next branch and pulled himself up on that one, too. Then just to be safe, he went up one more level. *That should be high enough,* he thought.

He looked down and saw the last few wolves run by the base of the tree. None of them even glanced in his direction. They sped by, their breathing hard and labored, as though they'd been running for a long time. But what could they be running from? Hunters? Maybe, but he doubted it. It would take a lot to scare a pack of wolves that size into running away.

Maybe it was something environmental. He sniffed the air, trying to detect any evidence of fire. But there was nothing. No smoke, no ash, just a calm serenity that felt eerily out of place in the valley at this time of year.

After waiting for about thirty minutes to make sure the wolves didn't return, he started to climb down the tree. He was about halfway down when the tree started to shake. A quick glance around told him other trees were shaking, too.

Another earthquake? That made two of them in as many days. What the hell was going on? He decided to wait this one out in the tree. After about five minutes, the earth stilled, and he climbed the rest of the way down.

He turned back toward his cave, forgetting about the spring and any deer that might be there. Odds were good the wolves would have scared them off, anyway. The walk back was filled with dark, worried thoughts about the coming winter.

One Day Left

The quake woke him up. He'd been dreaming about sailing on rough seas, which he'd never done, and when he woke up he found the rocking motion of the sea had been replaced by the violent rumbling and shaking of the ground underneath him. The whole cave pitched back and forth as though it were on a huge vibrating bed. Outside, rocks tumbled past the entrance, some small, others the size of full-grown black bears.

He got to his feet, determined not to be in the cave if the ceiling fell in, and lurched his way to the opening. Once there, he steeled his resolve and ran through the cascade of falling rocks, hoping to skate through without getting crushed.

A jagged rock the size of a softball grazed his shoulder, drawing a deep gash about four inches long, but he made it outside otherwise unharmed. Once he was clear of the entrance, he didn't stop, knowing that rocks and debris would cascade down the mountain as long as the ground continued to shake. He sprinted down the slope, hoping to find a safe point in the valley to wait out the quake.

He stumbled and fell more than once as the ground lurched and bucked underneath his feet. Rocks and tree limbs fell all around him like hail, but he managed to stay clear of the larger pieces. At one point a boulder the size of a small car rolled by, but he dove to the side just in time to avoid being turned into pulp. The boulder rumbled past, taking its own mini quake with it. Just as he thought he was safe a smaller stone clipped the side of his head and sent him to the ground in a spasm of vertigo and pain.

He lay there, about twenty feet off the valley floor, panting for breath. His lungs burned, and he knew he needed to get up, but he couldn't move. The pain in his hands faded as the new pain in his head took center stage. He sat up, and immediately vomited. He hadn't eaten much the night before, but that didn't stop his stomach from clenching and spewing a puddle of bile across the rocky ground. After the pain in his belly subsided and he could once again draw breath, he sat, dizzy and disoriented, waiting for the next big boulder to end his life.

And then, as if turned off by a light switch, the quake ended.

In the valley below, animals ran madly to the east. Bear, coyotes, rabbits, squirrels, and deer sped by, their eyes wide with fear. He even spotted a cougar speeding along the valley floor, heedless of the many morsels nearby it as it ran to safety. In the sky, clouds of birds blocked out the sun as they flew east, as well.

Where were they going?

More importantly, *why* were they going?

As he watched the endless parade of wildlife make tracks eastward, he came to a decision. The animals must know something he didn't. If they were running east, then by God, he would go, too.

He scanned the mountain's face. His home for the last fifteen years. He could just make out the entrance to his cave among the rubble. He'd need supplies, and all his supplies were in the cave. At bare minimum he'd need his knife and something to carry water. He could hunt with the knife, if he had to. He'd rather have his sling, of course, but at this point he'd take what he could get.

He climbed slowly back up to his cave. The climb took longer than normal because of the many cracks and rocks that had been displaced. In many places, his old route was completely covered up and he had to find other ways around. He stayed alert, not wanting to be caught off guard if another quake came, even though he knew there wasn't much point. He didn't have any place to go. If the earth started to shake again, he'd be pitched off the side of the mountain like a dislodged rock.

But the quakes didn't return, and aside from a few scrapes on his hands and elbows, he made it to the cave more or less unscathed. He looked up at the sun. Mid afternoon. Probably around 2 or 3 o'clock. The climb had taken him half a day. No wonder he was exhausted. Down in the valley, the animals continued their mad dash eastward. A pack of wolves padded by, leaving a group of quail in relative peace as the flightless birds made their own haste. He would be joining them soon, but he needed tools. And a weapon. Wherever those animals were going, they'd get hungry sooner or later. He had no intention of surviving an earthquake just to become dinner for a panicked bear or a starving band of coyotes.

The entrance to the cave was partially covered by rocks and pieces of broken trees, and he wasted another hour clearing an opening big enough for him to get through and take a few supplies with him. Once inside, he was surprised at how relatively unscathed the inside of the cave was. A few packs of dried meat had fallen off the wall, and a few small rocks had settled onto his pallet, but other than that it looked much like it was supposed to look.

I could have stayed in here and been just fine, he thought, rubbing the side of his head where the rock hit. The lump had grown to the size of a duck egg, and hurt to touch. He forced himself to remain still while he poured cold water into the wound, as well as the one on his shoulder. Then he wrapped both in strips of cloth he tore from his threadbare blanket. It wasn't much, but it would do the job.

His wounds tended, he grabbed two packs of dried meat and a canteen of water. The canteen held two quarts, which would be enough to get from one body of water to the next, at least until he reached the eastern foothills. Once there, he would be out of familiar territory and would have to search for water. He'd done it before, though, and he could do it again. His old leather sack hung on a wooden pike set into the floor, and he grabbed it, filling it with all the spare clothing he had left. If he were stuck outside in the coming winter, he'd need every scrap, and probably more. Finally, he grabbed his bow and three remaining arrows. They would be clumsy to carry, but he'd feel better having them along.

He squeezed his supplies through the opening, then pushed his way through the hole and out into the sunlight. The sun's position told him it was close to six o'clock. He only had a couple hours of daylight left. Better make the most of them.

Below him, the number of animals running east had thinned considerably. He didn't want to think about what that might mean. Using a strong, sturdy stick for balance, he set off down the slope. It had been a long time since he'd carried this much on his back, and his aching muscles and joints let him know they didn't appreciate the extra weight. He ignored the protests of his aging body.

Halfway down, and still a good eighty feet above the valley floor, he slipped in some loose rocks. Overbalanced by his heavy load, he was unable to correct himself, and tumbled over the edge. He saw the rock ledge below him, and braced for the impact.

There was a sudden, blinding flash of pain, then nothing at all.

Ash

He drifted slowly back to consciousness, more a gradual increase of awareness than actual clear thought. He didn't open his eyes, preferring the dark of his eyelids. His head throbbed, a constant pounding that threatened to make him nauseous again. He rolled onto his side and dry heaved. There was nothing in his stomach to expel.

Pain assaulted him from every angle. His head felt like it had split open. His arm screamed a fiery curse at the rest of his body, and his left leg felt broken. But if he didn't open his eyes, he could go back to sleep, and then the pain would go away.

Through the fog of dizziness and pain, he caught a strange smell in the air. It almost smelled like smoke, but not quite. It smelled more like ashes. As if the world had burned to death while he was unconscious. He didn't know what it meant, but it couldn't be good.

He tried to lose himself into the darkness again. But the more he tried, the more the pain kept him awake. Finally. He couldn't ignore it anymore, and he tried to open his eyes. The lids were stuck together by some gummy, sticky mess - probably blood - and he had to open them with the fingers on his good arm.

It took a moment for his eyes to focus. He lay on a rocky outcrop about twenty feet off the valley floor. He must have bounced along a little further down the slope after hitting the ledge. That would certainly account for the pain in his arm and leg, which shouted at him even louder now that he was conscious again. He had some herbs in his pack that might help, although if his leg were truly broken they wouldn't do much good. He'd need a splint, and he damn sure wasn't going anywhere for a while.

The world around him had a soft, gray quality, as though he'd awakened at dusk or early dawn. He could not see the sun through the haze. The sky was thick with gray clouds. And it was snowing.

Already? he thought. *It's not time yet. And it's nowhere near cold enough.*

He took another look, noting the dingy gray color of the flakes falling from the sky. Not snow, he realized, but something else.

One of the flakes landed on his forearm, and he noticed for the first time that there were hundreds of them covering his body.

Ash.

He brushed the ashes off his arm, immediately regretting it as another flare of pain shot through him. He almost screamed, but held it in, lest some hungry predators hear him and think about a nice, helpless meal.

He coughed. A thick wad of gray matter shot from his mouth to smack into the dingy tree to his right. Not good.

Down in the valley, no animals remained. As the ash piled up, it covered any tracks left behind by the stragglers.

It was getting harder and harder to breathe.

A shadow fell over the valley, and he looked up into the sky. The soft gray clouds had been replaced by an angry black wall.

More ash. Lots more.

He coughed again, his lungs trying desperately to clear themselves. *I should have just left with the animals,* he thought. *Too late, now.*

Then the black wall poured into the valley.

Shelter
by David Dalglish

Jason pushed aside the curtains to watch as the rumbling clouds neared. Melissa squirmed in his arms.

"Daddy, I'm scared," she said.

"We all are," he told her. "Sit still. This'll be pretty, I promise."

"I want to watch Spongebob," Melissa insisted.

"Not now," Jason said, his eyes wide as the sky suddenly cleared. Calm red sky shone above, clean, ominous. Then it was gone, a rolling black wall of cloud and ash sweeping over it.

"Daddy, Spongebob!"

Jason kissed the top of her head, wondering if she felt his tears dripping down. He'd give anything to send her to that underwater paradise forever. Instead, he had only his arms, his walls, and his love to offer. The house shook as wind slammed against it. The darkness deepened, broken only by thick bursts of lightning.

"Is it going to rain?" Melissa asked.

"No, sweetie," he said. "Not now."

Not ever.

*

It'd taken six rolls of duct tape, but Jason was confident he'd sealed the building. Every side of every window he'd layered. After locking and barring his front door, he'd stuffed old shirts into the crack below, then started taping. He lived in a modular home on his property not too far out of town. He thanked god it was fairly new. Last summer he'd looked at a two-story fixer-upper in the middle of town. The extra room would have been nice, but there'd been so many windows needing fixed, walls painted, and floors retiled that he'd passed. Sitting against the front door, a half-used roll of duct tape in hand, Jason couldn't imagine trying to seal that old place up.

Melissa sat on the couch, huddled under a mountain of pink princess blankets.

"Can we have candles?" she asked. "The dark is scary."

"We can't, babe," Jason said. "Air is precious now."

"When will the lights come back on?"

Jason sighed. He debated whether to lie or tell the truth. Biting down on his lower lip, he told the lie. In the darkness, unable to see her wide eyes, it came easy.

"In a week or two. We'll rough it until then. We're like pioneers. You read about pioneers in school, right?"

"They lived in dirt houses," Melissa said. "How'd they keep the bugs out?"

"They didn't," Jason said. "The bugs were their friends. They named them and built them little houses to live in beside their cabinets."

"Daddy!"

"What? They didn't teach you that in school?"

Jason smiled when he heard her laugh. Thank God for small miracles.

"Tell you what," he said. "You be a good girl and stay on the couch, and I'll get us a flashlight."

"Okay," she said, her voice muffled by the blankets.

Jason stretched out his arms and took baby steps toward the kitchen, feeling like a blind Frankenstein. Vague blobs grew in the darkness, outlines of the sink or the fridge. He stubbed his toe on a toy, something plastic with wheels. It rolled into kitchen, the sound grating. Without the television, air conditioners, his computer, cars outside, planes above, and water heater below, the resulting quiet was shocking. Sometimes the wind picked up, whipping against the side of his house. Other times the clouds grumbled in angry thunder. But mostly there was silence.

"You okay, dad?" Melissa asked him, sounding so far away.

"I'm fine," he said. "When the lights come on, you're cleaning up your toys."

She didn't respond, and inwardly he cursed himself. Why'd he have to remind her of what they didn't have?

His hand brushed the counter. He used it to guide himself along until reaching a drawer he'd purposefully left open. Inside was a handful of flashlights. He grabbed one of the smaller ones and clicked it on. The white microwave shone into view for half a second before he shut it back off. Tempting as it was, he kept it off on his way back to the couch.

"Where you at?" he asked when he felt his toes bump the couch's edge. "Come on, let's see, where you hiding?"

He waved his arms around him blindly, and when his fingers brushed blanket, he dove them forward, his fingers tickling. Giggles rewarded his efforts.

"St-stop!" Melissa shouted.

Jason plopped down next to her. He felt her slide closer, her head pressed against his chest.

"You got the flashlight?" she asked.

In answer he aimed it at her face and flicked it twice.

"Dad!" she grumbled, elbowing him. Jason chuckled, then flipped it around in his hand.

"So you still scared?" he asked her.

"A little," she said.

"Of what? Are there monsters?"

Melissa snorted, as if she were insulted. She was six: way too old to be believing in monsters. It was ghosts she was afraid of.

"I think there's something in the corner," she said.

"Which corner?"

"That corner."

Jason waited a moment.

"Dear, are you pointing?"

Melissa giggled.

"Maybe."

Jason aimed the flashlight and flicked it on for a half-second, revealing their coat rack.

"No monsters there," he said.

"Not there!"

He switched places, flicking the light off and on as he continued his elusive search.

"Any monsters there? How about there? Oops, none there, either. What are we looking for again?"

Melissa's tiny fingers jabbed into his sides and under his arms. Jason laughed, swinging the flashlight down so he could see her face. She smiled up at him, wincing at the bright light. Her hair was a dark mess, wet strands clinging to her cheeks. She was smiling, but it was fragile and trembling. A dammed ocean of tears swirled within her. Come bedtime, he knew she'd let them loose.

"You're so beautiful," he said, letting the light linger so he could burn the image into his mind. "I'll be beating the boys away with a stick when you hit high school."

He flicked off the light. Melissa sniffled, so he wrapped his arms around her and held her close.

"Is mom alright?" she asked after their silence stretched for several minutes.

Jason thought of his ex-wife's phone call. Karen had been at the office when the news hit.

"It's only an hour drive," she'd insisted. "I'll be back in time, alright? Just please, don't go anywhere. Promise me, Jason."

"I won't," he'd said.

"Promise."

"Alright, I promise."

The drive from her office to his house normally took an hour, but Jason imagined the frantic drivers, the wrecks, the police squads and rioters. When the clouds hit, she'd most likely been in her car, her windows flimsy protection against the tiny granules of ash that poured into her lungs, solidified, and killed her.

Jason kissed Melissa's fingers.

"She's fine," he said. "She's just late in joining us."

Thunder rolled.

"She's with God in heaven, isn't she?" Melissa asked.

Jason's eyes ran with tears. He felt his lower lip tremble. He clutched his daughter to his chest and fought the trembling of his voice.

"I hope so," he told her. "I really do."

Melissa broke, same as he. In the darkness they cried.

*

Once Melissa was asleep, Jason shifted her to the side and stood. He flicked on the flashlight, wincing at its brightness. Knowing there was nothing so important as this, he calmly and patiently checked the tape. In the thin stream of light, any ash sneaking through would be readily visible. He saw none at the door, nor his bathroom window.

The kitchen had a tiny bit puffing in on one side. An extra layer of duct tape put an end to that. The back door had a bit more coming in, and he smelled the distinct odor of sulfur. Jason used two layers on that one, then sat and watched. Bits of everyday household dust floated before him, but no more ash pushed through the cracks. He wiped a bit of cold sweat from his forehead and continued.

When finished, Jason was satisfied. A little bit of ash might still be filtering in, but nowhere near enough to cause them any immediate danger. It might give him cancer twenty years down the road, but hell, he'd accept the compromise.

In his living room, just beside his computer desk, was a giant window facing west. Jason pulled back the curtain. Outside he saw only darkness. He pressed his fingers to the glass, shocked by the cold. Summer was in mid-swing, but sweltering heat waves were years from returning. He wished he'd bought a gas generator like he'd always wanted to. Too late now. Everything was too late.

He shone his light through the window and stared. Even though he was wasting batteries, he couldn't make himself shut it off.

"Is it snowing?" he heard Melissa ask from the couch. Jason startled at the sound of her voice.

"It is," he said. "But it's warm snow. You wouldn't like it."

"Doesn't feel warm," Melissa said. "It's cold in here."

"Stay under the blankets," he told her. "I'll join you in a moment."

Thick flakes of ash fell through his beam of light, drifting lazily downward. Everything he saw was covered in a thin layer of gray and white. The sight was oddly beautiful. He felt a bit uneasy watching it fall. It was too gray, he decided. It lacked the purity of snow. More worrisome was the way it covered the ground. Every blade of grass, every flower, lay crumpled flat by the weight. A heavy snow. A killing snow.

He shut off the flashlight.

*

Jason's watch claimed it was half past nine, but still the outside remained dark. Slowly he rubbed his eyes and tried to convince his body daytime had arrived. Melissa had awoken every couple of hours throughout the night, crying hysterically and asking for her mother. The first few times Jason had whispered to her, telling stories and zapping monsters with his flashlight. The final time he'd simply held her and silently cried.

"You hungry?" he asked as he pushed the blankets off and stood.

"I guess," Melissa said.

He didn't turn on the flashlight until he reached the kitchen. Opening and closing cabinet doors, he looked for what might go bad first. The most obvious was the cereal, sickly sweet and coated with sugar. He poured two great bowls and opened the refrigerator. He yanked out the milk, hoping to keep in the cold for as long as possible. Food coloring from the marshmallows swirled the milk red and pink as Jason poured. Popping on the lid, he flung it back into the fridge, closed it with his hip, and then plopped two spoons into the bowls.

"Soup's up," he said, his voice muffled by the flashlight in his teeth. He carried a bowl in each hand. By the time he set them down upon the table, his jaw ached. Flicking the flashlight about, he shone it near Melissa's bowl until she sat down before it. With a click, he shut it off.

"I can't see," she whined.

"You can eat cereal in the dark," he said. "Not rocket science."

"You would say that," Melissa muttered.

The cereal was far from his favorite, but Jason ate every bit. His search through the cabinets hadn't been very hopeful. Much of what he had, things like macaroni, spaghetti, and noodles, needed boiled. Thankfully he had cans of soup, which would help a ton. There was plenty of juice and soda in his fridge, which would last far longer than the milk. He'd tried the faucet only once, and the gray smudge that spurted out was certainly nothing he planned on drinking.

Milk dribbling down his chin, Jason wiped it with his arm and then let out a weak burp. A few moments later,

Melissa responded in kind. Her giggles were far brighter in their gray world than any flashlight.

Above them, the roof creaked.

*

Jason told stories to pass the time.

"One day, papa bunny left the rabbit hole in search of a carrot," he said. Melissa sat curled beside him, shivering under the blankets. Every hint of summer had bled out through the walls. Frost lined the inside of the windows, ash the outside.

"A big carrot?" asked Melissa.

"Biggest there ever was. And he knew where to get it, too. Old farmer Rick had this prize carrot, but he guarded it with dogs and an electric fence. But papa bunny really wanted that carrot for mama bunny. It'd feed them through the winter. Such a carrot was a dream come true. So every day he went to the garden, testing fences, racing the dogs. Every day he came back tired and worn, but still no carrot."

"This is a sad story," Melissa said.

"Sometimes stories are sad," Jason said.

He stared at where the television hid in the darkness, thinking how much easier it had once made their lives. His daughter squirmed beside him.

"Well, what happened?" she asked.

"Papa bunny finally figured out a way to get that carrot. He outran the dogs. He outsmarted the farmer. He dug that carrot up and ran home, dragging it by its leafy top. But mama bunny wasn't there. Papa bunny had been gone so long, she forgot who he was and wandered off. The carrot was so big, papa bunny couldn't eat it by himself. It rotted, and it stank, and he couldn't clean the smell out of the walls. So he left their rabbit hole forever. The end."

"Is that what happened to you and mom?" Melissa asked.

He kissed her forehead.

"It's just a story, sweetheart," he told her.

*

L unch was another bowl of cereal. For dinner, Jason pulled out a bag of frozen meatballs and let them thaw on the counter. After a couple of hours, they were soft enough to eat.

"Just imagine them surrounded with spaghetti," Jason said. "All slippery and warm."

"I hate spaghetti."

"Spaghetti hates you too," he said.

They slept together on the couch, their bellies full. Jason had chased what little thirst they had with a few sips of soda. Things were going to get worse, but at least they had plenty to eat while things were roughest outside. All throughout the night, the ceiling cracked and groaned.

Come the morning, Jason pulled back the giant curtain in the living room.

"Hot damn!" he shouted, an idiot smile tugging at the corners of his mouth. Melissa stirred and rubbed her eyes. Without a flashlight, he saw her do so, and he laughed again. Pouring in through the window was a dim gray light. Starlight was brighter, but compared to the thick cave-like darkness, nothing could have been more beautiful. Melissa joined her father's side and took his hand. Together, they looked out upon the lawn.

The ash still fell, a death snow killing every blade of grass, smothering every flower, and coating every vehicle. Jason guessed at least two inches, if not more. The wind picked up, and the air clogged with thin, sand-like gusts of ash.

"Can we go out and play?" Melissa asked.

"It still isn't safe," Jason said. "Once it stops...snowing, we can try to get out. We'll wear masks over our face, like ski masks. You know when your grandma smokes, and it smells bad and hurts to breathe in? It's like that out there, just worse."

"Nothing's worse than grandma's smokes," Melissa insisted. "Except maybe Mark's breath. It smells like boogers."

Jason laughed on instinct. His heart wasn't in it. Most likely grandma was dead. He'd tried not to think about it, but he saw little hope. Would anyone stay with the elderly in a nursing home after hearing the news? Perhaps a few would. He wanted to think that. But he knew otherwise. Hell, even that Mark kid was probably gone, packed into a car and driven east in a frantic bid for safety.

"I'm sure Mark's breath is bad," he said, turning and coughing to hide his wipe at his eyes. "Still, out there is worse. That's why we're staying inside. We're safe here. We have shelter."

Jason went through and opened all the curtains. He knew what little heat they had would escape faster, but right then it seemed light was more crucial to life than warmth. Just in case, he threw on another sweater and zipped Melissa up in a jacket. They ate the last of the cereal, then scrounged around for some games. Jason pushed aside his computer desk so they had plenty of room to play by the window.

"Your computer," Melissa said as it toppled over. "Don't you need it?"

Jason only laughed.

They played checkers, Candyland, and a Spongebob game whose rules Melissa seemed to understand more than Jason did. They moved around markers, bumped into each other, took turns tickling one another, and then finally finished with a great roaring campfire song. Melissa giggled in his arms. She noticed the puffs of white every time she exhaled, so she put two fingers to her mouth and then blew.

"Look, I'm granny," she said.

A loud crack startled them both. Jason lurched to the window, wiping at the frost in hopes of seeing what made the noise. It didn't matter. The ash was too thick on the other side.

"What happened?" Melissa asked.

"It sounded like glass," Jason said. "I'm not sure what."

"Can you go look?" she asked.

Jason shook his head, then thumped it against the glass. A bit of the ash fell. Rolling his eyes, Jason slapped his hand against the glass, scattering more of the ash. He saw the cause immediately. The back window of his car had collapsed inward, thick ash pouring into the back seat. He bit his lip, wondering if maybe a large rock from the eruption had struck his car.

No, he thought, shaking his head. That was dumb. He knew what had happened. He'd just hoped otherwise. The ash was rock, thin rock, but rock nonetheless. Once it settled, it was like concrete, and two inches was more than enough to slowly crack and break the glass.

"What was it?" Melissa asked. She joined his side and looked out at the land of ash. "Someone throw a rock?"

"Maybe," he said. "Come on. Let's have a rematch at that checkers game. I think you cheated."

"Did NOT," she insisted.

He stole one last glance outside before sitting down. Trees lined the edge of his property, their branches hung low as if bowing in deference to the darkened sky.

*

Jason awoke to the sound of screeching metal. He rolled off the couch, banging his elbow on the table and scattering checker pieces. Melissa startled, her blankets pulled about her, her cry piercing the darkness.

"Shit," said Jason as he clutched his elbow and sucked in his breath. He fumbled about for the flashlight. From the far side of the house, metal shrieked again, coupled with a sudden roaring of wind.

"Daddy, I'm scared, make it stop!" cried Melissa.

Jason felt the touch of plastic and curled his fingers about it. As the light flicked on, he aimed it toward the door.

"It's alright, babe," he said. "Daddy's going to see what the matter is, all right?"

"What's going on?" she asked. The sound of metal died down, but the wind remained.

"Something happened in my bedroom. You stay here and be a brave girl, okay?"

As he stepped into the kitchen, the light of his flashlight aimed toward his bedroom door, he heard Melissa sob. Feeling like an idiot, he retrieved a second flashlight from a drawer and brought it to her. He clicked it on and shone it at her hands.

"No monsters can survive a flashlight's touch," he told her, kissing her forehead.

"Or ghosts?"

"Not ghosts, either."

She hugged the flashlight to her chest and looked at him, trying so hard to be brave.

"Okay. I'm all right now, dad."

He smiled even as his heart pounded in his chest. He'd seen the bedroom door for just a brief moment, but there was no mistaking the streams of ash billowing in through the cracks. Grabbing a roll of duct tape, he went back into the kitchen. Pausing before the door, his hand on the knob, he closed his eyes and prayed.

Please, God, don't be what I think it is. Anything but that.

He shoved open the door. He looked inside. He closed the door.

"Fuck you, God," he said.

Jason layered all four sides with duct tape, using an entire roll. The whole while, he coughed and punched the wood. He knew he must be scaring Melissa, but he didn't care. Nothing mattered. The ceiling had collapsed, broken under the weight of the heavy ash. His fists pounded the door, and he flung the empty roll toward the overflowing trash bin. As he sobbed, he saw a beam of light from the living room circling about. Wiping his face, he followed it, feeling like a lost ship tracking a lighthouse.

Navigating the rocky course of toys, game boards, and table, Jason fell to his knees and wrapped Melissa in his arms. He felt her pat his head as if he were one of her dolls.

"You okay, daddy?" she asked. "You okay?"

He held her tighter.

*

"Don't we need to save food?" she asked. Jason only smiled. He'd cracked open a can of ravioli, the sauce thick and cold. They took turns dipping in their spoons and slurping the stuff down. The living room had taken on a gray hue from the dim light piercing the windows.

"Think Spongebob has room for us in his pineapple?" he asked her.

"Stop being silly."

Outside, glass shattered, coupled with a sound of bending metal. Melissa jumped.

"What was that?" she asked.

"Just the car," Jason said, dipping his spoon into the can and scooping out the bottom. "Just the dumb old car. You packed?"

Melissa nodded.

David Dalglish

"I have everything," she said.

"Let me see."

Beside her lay a pink backpack she'd taken with her to first grade. He unzipped it and reached in his hand. He pulled out a Barbie doll, the checkerboard and its pieces, a box of cookies, two flashlights, and a teddy bear.

"Yup," Jason said, kissing her nose. "That's everything."

They both wore layers of shirts and pants, plus ski caps and winter coats. Jason hoisted his own backpack, filled with food, flashlights, bottles of water, and a gun. He set it down on the couch and went to the kitchen, returning holding several washcloths.

"Now this is very important," Jason said. "Probably the most important thing ever, alright? You keep this across your face at all times, and never breathe through anything other than the cloth. You understand, sweetie?"

"Yeah."

He tied a yellow cloth around her face, double-knotting it behind her head. When he stood, she looked up at him, her eyes sparkling with wonder. While she watched, he tied one around his own face.

"We're going out there, aren't we?" Melissa asked. "Into the warm snow?"

Jason chuckled.

"We are."

He ripped the tape off the sides of the front door, curling it up into a giant sticky wad. Once enough was gone, he grabbed the door knob and pulled. Biting air swirled in, angry in its cold. Ash stung their eyes, and already Jason fought a cough.

"You ready?" he asked. Melissa nodded.

Hand in hand, they abandoned their shelter.

43

Beach Puppies
By Daniel Arenson

They sat on the beach, beers in hands, on the night their island ended.

"There goes another one," Sean whispered, gazing into the sky where a jet plane, headlights cutting through the darkness, airlifted another five hundred refugees to safety. "Seventy-third since we got here."

Harvey watched his friend. Sean was a small man, rail thin, a man whose round glasses and goatee made him look like a fiery intellectual--an island Trotsky, if you will--but Harvey still remembered him as that scrawny kid the bullies picked on. Sean had always loved numbers, as a child prodigy and now as a professor of number theory, and today he was the only one counting.

In fact, Harvey thought, he was the only one watching at all. He had always been the nervous one, Sean.

Jess and Mike, now, they were your happy couple. Yes, they stretched out on their futons, ran their toes through the sand, and laughed between bottles of beer. Mike had his shirt off, revealing a tattoo of the Cheshire Cat climbing his arm. Jess wore jean shorts and a bikini top, sporting tattoos of ten dark roses, her flower of the night. She punched Mike, who laughed and took another swig of beer. She lit a joint, passed it to him, and their laughter grew.

Looking at them, Harvey thought, you'd never know the fire was coming. Or maybe you *would* know. Maybe that was exactly how you should look on the night you, your friends, your entire island died.

"Hell," Jess said and tossed an empty bottle into the waves ahead, those waves whispering in the darkness, only their foamy crests visible in the night. "We gonna die tonight, right? So we die laughing, eh?"

"Damn right!" Mike said, raising a bottle for this Pacific jewel, this dying land. He emptied it, tried to throw it into the water, but hit his foot instead. Jess howled with laughter. Around them puppies scampered, pets abandoned by their owners, those owners airlifted overhead. The pups were happy too, unaware that they were sacrificed to fire; ignorance, like booze, was bliss.

Harvey envied Mike and Jess, as he'd always envied their spirit, their carelessness, their ability to stare the world in the face and tell it to go to hell. They did that now too, just instead of giving the world the finger, they thrust it up at death. For them, life had always been a party. Death was just its final bash.

And there, behind this laughing couple, sat David. He was smiling softly. His hair was long, his face unshaven. Watercolors stained his pants, for David was the artist among them, their seeker of colors and life. He raised his eyes to the full moon, and his smile widened as he saw the birds that fled.

"Doves," he said. "I haven't seen doves in so long."

Yes, for David, this last night was for beauty. In his eyes, he saw only the moonlight on the water, the seashells glinting on the sand, the puppies that played around them.

Harvey envied them all: David, for finding these last glimmers of beauty; Jess and Mike, for being so happy or shallow; Sean, for his intelligence, his perfect understanding of their place in history, the significance of these planes that keep roaring overhead.

Because, Harvey thought, *I feel nothing.*

"Eighty-four," Sean whispered, watching from behind those round glasses, and Harvey watched the plane too. It was low enough to see clearly, even in the dark, and Harvey thought of the people inside, the people who'd won the raffle. The people who'd won life.

He looked at his friends. The unfortunate. The lottery losers. The dying.

For the first time that evening, Harvey smiled, because he loved them and even though his insides quivered, he knew there was no better way to die.

He had always held them together, hadn't he? Not quite their leader, no, but... maybe their glue. Harvey reached into his pocket and felt the paper there. His winning ticket. His plane ticket out. The possibility of life in the remnants of the freezing world.

Harvey closed his eyes. *Not without them.* He crumbled the paper in his fist, pulled it from his pocket, and tossed it to the water. In the darkness, he couldn't see it disappear in the ocean. It was better that way.

"One hundred," Sean soon said, barely audible over the joking and singing of the happy, drunk couple. "I think that's the last one."

Harvey took a swig of beer when he noticed that not only planes blotted the stars. A darkness spread in the east, moving fast, like tar spilled across the sky.

"Hey, I heard a good one the other night," Jess said, bottle in hand. "A rabbi and a priest walk into a bar, and...."

The roar of ash soon drowned out her voice, and Harvey turned his eyes away. He looked at the beach puppies and smiled as the darkness and fire came crashing down.

Toward the Storm
by David Dalglish

It was always storming to the northwest. Gertrude decided that was why she struggled to maintain a cheery attitude through the long, dreary day. Before the ash had swept across her Kentucky home, she'd been bright as the morning sun when hosting potlucks and meeting with their church choir, of which she had been the undisputed leader. Now she walked with a stoop, her skin a permanent gray, her hair a scraggly stiff mess no comb had a hell's chance of fixing. Every day, she travelled west, toward the forever looming gray wall.

Through her weeks of travel, Gertrude had made it to I-44. She almost felt like laughing sometimes when she looked around her. Before, she'd always been too scared to drive on the interstate, not feeling comfortable going above fifty, let alone anywhere near the ninety it seemed the other drivers wished her to go. Now she had it all to herself, and at walking speed no less. Vehicles rested on the sides, some wrecked, most not. When the ash had hit, the cars, trucks, and semis had sputtered and stalled, their engines ruined and their drivers blinded.

"Oh goodness," Gertrude said, coming upon a particularly vicious wreck. A small sportscar lay perpendicular to the road. Sprawled further ahead was an ash-covered lump, most certainly a body. Gertrude wiped a hand across the twisted metal, cleaning away until she could see the color.

"Always red," Gertrude said, her voice muffled by the thick scarf she wore wrapped around her face. "The careless ones always drive red. A smart driver picks blue."

She peered through the broken windows, looking for anything useful. A suitcase lay half-open on the floor, full of clothes, a broken laptop beside it. Gertrude shook her head. Careless and ill-prepared. She doubted she'd have gotten along with him when he was alive.

"May God be kinder toward you than I would ever be," she said to the lump as she walked on by. If there was one thing good about the ash, it was how it slowly, steadily buried the dead. That was just like God. He'd made his mess, and now he was helping to clean it up.

Gertrude walked with no particular haste, just fast enough to keep herself warm. She had a second scarf wrapped about her hair, two thick jackets, a sweater, long underwear, and tall black boots. Little of it matched, but that also mattered none. Once the world wiped it gray, it all matched. The clothing kept her warm enough, though come nightfall she'd still need a fire to keep the chill out of her old bones.

The next vehicle she came upon looked more promising, although every vehicle had potential. At times she closed her eyes and pretended she was garage-sailing, seeking out bargains with every stop. You never knew what you might find if you looked hard enough.

"Going to put you down now, Alice," Gertrude said. She removed the strap to her thick pack from around her neck and set it upon the street. Her 'garage', a proper family car that turned out to be dark green, parked on the far side of the curb. After she struck the sides to break away chunks of ash, she opened the door, her hand over her nose. Sometimes the people remained within, rotted and bloated because they were and hidden from God's burial snow. Thankfully, the car was empty. The family inside must have abandoned it in a mad attempt to walk to safety.

Gertrude found the button for the trunk underneath the steering wheel and pressed it. She heard a click. The trunk didn't open immediately, waiting for her to clear off the excess weight atop it. Once free, it flipped open. The old woman stared greedily at the blankets and grocery bags. Evidently the family had stocked far more than they could carry. By her estimate, she could stay at least three nights before moving on. Excellent.

"I count two blankets," she said to Alice. "Some canned food...let's see here. Corn. Green beans. Spaghettios. Ooh, some pudding, how wonderful! Doubt I'll find some cat food, but this, let me look, yes, this should do. Spam!"

From within the pack, a small feline head stuck out and looked around. It sneezed twice and then retreated back into warmth and safety. Gertrude grinned at it from behind her scarf. Alice was very calm for a cat. She slept in the pack, relaxing during the day while Gertrude walked. At night she cuddled on her chest for warmth and ate a little of the food Gertrude set out for her.

"Hrm, what else do we have?" Gertrude asked, her busy hands carefully adjusting the contents of the trunk. "If there's food, then there is always a little bit of...well fiddlesticks. No water, Alice. We might have to move out sooner than I hoped."

She shut the trunk and returned to the front, not at all worried that Alice might slip out and run away. Inside the car were a few more possessions, which Gertrude rifled through with numb fingers. Part of her wondered what the family had been like. Had they been good church-going folk, on their knees every Sunday like God expected? Or perhaps they were the football-worshipping type, more likely to cheer at a touchdown than God's daily miracles come his day of rest?

Gertrude found a child-seat strapped in the back. Her lips quivered, and shaking her head she struck her breast.

"Forgive me, God," she said. "It's wrong of me to judge. Your job, not mine, and old Gertrude Henderson isn't much good at anything to dare take your place."

She leaned back inside and moved a jacket. As if in reward for her prayer, she found a six-pack of bottled water resting on the floor. Tears welled in her eyes, but she quickly wiped them away. The land was too hard for tears. She had to remain upbeat, positive.

"We got water!" Gertrude shouted to Alice. "Hallelujah! Let's make us a fire!"

*

Gertrude claimed one of the blankets, then piled the remaining two together behind the car. She sat on its eastern side, using it to block the wind. Night was falling, and while it looked like a storm, it was hard to tell. Clouds forever billowed from the west, and even though she marched toward them every day, they never seemed to come closer. Sure, a piece of it might break off and rage eastward, rumbling with thunder but always withholding its rain. But the vast wall always stayed still.

One of the things she had the most of were lighters. It seemed every other car had at least one stored in their glove compartments. Gertrude would be no cavemen, not as long as she traveled her precious highway. Toward the storm, not away, that was the key.

"God doesn't reward those who run from their troubles," Gertrude told Alice as she used a lighter to set the remaining blankets aflame. For hundreds of miles, trees lined the outer edge of the interstate, sometimes near, sometimes far. With so much ash weighing down their branches, most had collapsed or snapped in half. Finding kindling and logs for fire was never difficult, just sometimes tiresome. But the treeline was particularly close that night, so she had extra firewood lined up beside the tire of the car.

Once the blankets were going good, she tossed on the branches and huddled closer. She opened the top of her pack, letting Alice come out on her own terms. She pet the cat a few times as she reached inside, then pulled out one of her most treasured possessions: a can opener. Not one of those modern plastic pieces of crap that Gertrude hated, either. It was an old fashioned can opener, made of steel and requiring only the strength of her hands to work. The ones with knobs and gears always seemed to warp and break on her. Not this one. Not her Trusty.

"Not nothing Trusty can't open," she said as she placed a can of Spaghettios near the fire. Using the tip of the can opener, she punched a hole at the top to make sure it didn't rupture or get too hot. Alice poked out her head, looked around, and then leapt free. She seemed perfectly suited to the land of ash, her fur solid gray but for many white lines running along her ribs and tail. The cat curled up beside the fire and lay still.

"Don't sleep too deep," Gertrude said. "Supper's almost ready."

She reached into her pack and pulled out a small ziplock bag. Inside were two spoons, three knives, and a fork. She unzipped the bag, retrieved the spoon, and then quickly closed it and stashed it in her pack. More than anything, she wanted her silverware clean. There was enough ash everywhere in the world; the least she could do was keep it out of her food.

Gertrude didn't lower her scarf to eat until she'd pulled up the sides of her coat, hunkering down away from the wind. Now that the burial snow had ceased falling, and the initial storms had passed, it seemed much safer to breathe the open air, but Gertrude never risked herself any longer than she needed to. Her lungs were old, and more importantly, they were the only pair she had. No sense in ruining them while they still worked.

Once a bit of steam trickled out the hole in the can, Gertrude pulled it away and let it cool for a moment. While she did, she retrieved one of the pudding cups. She felt like a giddy schoolgirl as she held it. How long had it been since she'd tasted a real dessert? Two weeks? Three? No matter. She'd taste one now, but only after eating! Trusty did its work on the rest of the lid, and then she wolfed down the Spaghettios, red sauce dripping down her chin. After that, she made quick work of the pudding. Between the two, she felt just like a child.

"Oh, I almost forgot about you," Gertrude said, dumping the last bits of sauce and noodle out beside the cat. "I seem to do that lately, don't I?"

She didn't remember if she'd fed Alice the night before, but it didn't seem to matter. Alice gave her a look that said, very clearly, 'You woke me up for this?' The cat laid her head back down and closed her eyes. Gertrude chuckled.

"Fine, you be that way. I'm…I'm…quite fine without you, thank you very much! Hrmph."

She decided she deserved another pudding cup before curling up beside the fire and drifting off to sleep under a mountain of blankets.

*

When she awoke, the night remained deep, and her fire roared healthily. A figure sat opposite of her, cracking some branches in his hands and throwing them onto the flame.

Gertrude screamed.

"Shit, lady!" the figure, a man, shouted. He stood and took a step back, as if worried she were dangerous. Gertrude kicked and squirmed until her back was against the car. Underneath her blankets, she clutched a steak knife, the one she slept with every night for the past three weeks.

"Go away!" Gertrude yelled. "Take – take – whatever you want, take. Go! Leave!"

"Stop screaming at me!" the man yelled back.

"No!"

The man sighed and rubbed his hand against his eyes. He sat back down. Gertrude shrunk deeper into her blankets at the sight of him. His face was ashen, his eyes sunken deep into his skull. A newly-grown beard curled around his chin. His hair was long and dark. When he smiled, his teeth were crooked.

"I'm not here to rob you, woman," he said. "My name is Samuel."

He waited. As if from a distant life, Gertrude remembered her firmly entrenched standards of politeness.

"Ms. Gertrude Henderson," she said. She pulled down her scarf so she didn't look like one of those women from the Middle East they sometimes showed on the news. "A pleasure to meet you, mister, assuming you aren't here to take my things."

"Might have been a time in my life I would have done just that," Samuel said. He smiled at her, but it reminded her of a wolf's smile, all teeth and lolling tongue. Except he looked tired, so tired. "But not now. Doesn't feel much point to it. The world's changing. Think we should be changing with it."

"A sensible thing to do," Gertrude said. She looked around. "What'd you do with Alice?"

"Alice?" asked Samuel.

"My cat."

The man shrugged.

"Haven't seen a cat. I've eaten a couple on the trip here, though. That meat's tough as nails. No good. Your cat is safe with me, miss."

Gertrude shot him a look that showed she very much doubted that. Samuel coughed and tossed another log onto the fire.

"So where you headed?" he asked.

Gertrude slowly put the knife down on the ground beside her, still hidden by her blankets. Pulling a hand free, she pointed west, following the highway.

"Well, I keep traveling that way, just me and Alice. You're the first I've seen in…blast this old memory. A week? Two? They weren't going my way, either. Nice people, good people. But they don't know what's smart to do!"

"And what is that?" asked Samuel. His face flickered in the light of the fire.

"Go west," Gertrude said, grinning wide. "People keep breaking into homes, but that's not where the food is. It ain't in the stores, neither. The cars, Samuel! I look in the cars because that's where people ran when they heard. They stole and they hid and they grabbed everything and then tried to drive away. I'm following the food."

"Toward the storm?" Samuel asked.

Gertrude nodded, her head bobbing rapidly up and down.

"Everyone went the other way. Such a gosh-darned gaggle of people, can't think they'll have but each other to eat soon! But no one's west. Just me. And you, I see, not that I expect you to keep coming with me. You're going east, aren't you, young man?"

"And if I am?" he asked.

"Then I should say goodbye, shouldn't I?" She laughed. "And good luck too, of course. We all could use a bit of luck, even with God keeping his eye so close."

Samuel shifted as if uncomfortable.

"Why's that?" he asked.

"What?"

"God keeping his eye close on us."

Gertrude gestured about wildly.

"Why, there's so much fewer of us to watch, ain't there? Guess everyone might be raising a din up in heaven to distract him, but I don't know that and neither do you!"

Samuel chuckled.

"What if," he said, letting his voice trail off for a moment. "What if I were actually going west instead of east?" he asked.

"Was that where you were going before tonight?" she asked. "You been following me?"

"No," he said, chuckling. "I was going east, but I'm thinking of changing directions now that I've met you. Is that all right with you, miss?"

"Ms. Henderson," she snapped. "If you're to call me a miss, you might as well use the name meant to go with it."

His smile faded for an instant, then returned, as if a cloud had passed over his face.

"But you called me mister," he said.

"That's because you told me nothing more," she said.

Gertrude looked about, her lips twitching.

"Now where'd Alice run off to?" she asked. "Alice? Alice! Come on back, girl. Silly, stupid cat. She'll be back by morning. Now if you excuse me, Samuel, I should get back to sleeping. I don't know how you are for food, but I have a bit to share come morning. Until then, good night. You're welcome to share the fire, especially since you got it going so well."

She curled back up under her blankets, her arm for a pillow, her knife for a teddy bear.

Samuel picked at his teeth, watching her sleep.

"Gertrude," he said.

"What?" she snapped.

"There's a question I'll need to ask you," he said, biting down on a fingernail. "But I won't ask you it just yet. I like travelling with you, you understand?"

Gertrude didn't, but she nodded anyway. It seemed like what he wanted, as well as the easiest way to get some shuteye. Just before she drifted off, she felt Alice pawing on her blankets, as if massaging her to sleep.

*

Gertrude startled awake come morning, jerking upward and letting out a soft cry. Samuel was already up, and his arms jolted, nearly dropping the bundle of wood he carried.

"Oh, morning," she said, acting as if nothing were the matter. "Surprised to see you up. Old bones, I guess. Used to be I was up in my apartment before any of the other youngsters. Funny dreams. Funny times."

"Morning," Samuel said. "I thought to keep the fire going throughout the day. The wind picked up while you slept. Today will be a cold one."

"Fire won't do us no good," Gertrude said as she tightened the scarf about her face and slowly disentangled herself from the blankets. "We can't stay here to enjoy it. With you here, I don't have enough food and water. That is, unless you brought your own."

"I have very little," Samuel admitted.

"Thought so," she said. "Now put your back to the car and keep your eyes to yourself. I need to pass water, and I won't have a funny-fuddy watching me go."

Samuel did as he was told, slowly shaking his head as she left. When he heard her footsteps, he turned back around. He held up a can of spam, the top popped open.

"Thought some hot breakfast might do us both good," he said.

"Thoughtful," she said. "You made sure it ain't spoiled, right?"

"Spam don't spoil," he replied.

Gertrude thought it did, but she decided not to argue. The top still on, Samuel tossed the spam into the middle of the fire for it to cook. He found another can of Spaghettios and tossed it in as well. Gertrude retrieved two bottles of water. She handed one to Samuel, and opened the other. Grabbing a small tin from within her pack, she set it on the ground and poured a bit of the water into it. Alice poked her head out from the pack, meowed, and then went over for a drink.

"Good girl," Gertrude said as she leaned back and watched. Samuel raised an eyebrow at her but said nothing.

At Samuel's insistence, they mixed the contents of the spam and Spaghettios together, adding a bit of flavor to each. It almost felt like cooking, something Gertrude ached to do again. Nothing made her feel alive like being amid a mess of flour, salt, tomatoes, and pasta. Reading a recipe correctly was an art, and she considered herself devoted to the craft.

"So what do you miss?" she asked Samuel as they ate.

"What?" he asked.

"Miss. Since this mess started. Anything you miss in particular?"

Samuel took a big bite from the can, using a spoon of his own he'd pulled out of his pocket. He chewed on it, both the question and the spoonful.

"Toilet paper," he said.

"You trying to make me blush?" Gertrude said, slapping his shoulder and laughing. "Good heavens, that's what you miss? I'd love to bake a nice lasagna and share it with my choir. I wish I could watch my soaps again, see those handsome men fighting with each other over gals I could only dream of being as pretty as. But you? Toilet paper. Your mind is in the gutter, mister."

"Just the practical," Samuel said. "Always have."

"A dull way to live."

He gave her a strange look at that, as if he were aware of a great secret that hung right before her nose. She bit her lips, swallowed one more spoonful of spamghettios, as Samuel called them, and then set the can down.

"Between the two of us, we can carry most of what's left," she said.

"I say we wait," Samuel said. "A storm is coming, a real one. Can't you feel it in the air?"

Gertrude rubbed her bony knuckles. Her arthritis was flaring like the devil, but it could mean plenty of things besides a storm. But the air had an energy to it, and the wind blew cold and full of promise.

"I haven't seen rain since the ash," she said. "Was starting to think it couldn't happen."

"Might not still," Samuel said. "But should it hit, I'm thinking it'd be best if we had shelter."

He nodded at the car. Gertrude glanced around to look at it, then shrugged.

"By golly, I guess we can use that when it comes down to it." She reached into her pack and stroked Alice on the head. "You won't mind being in there, will you, Alice? In where it'll stay nice and dry?"

Samuel hid his laugh with a cough.

*

The storm came on sudden and strong. Gertrude sat in the front passenger seat, her pack on her lap. Samuel sat in the back. Just before the winds picked up, he'd cleaned the windows, saying he was determined to watch.

The sky darkened, the light fading as if they were in the center of an eclipse. The wind beat against the car, howling as it slipped through unseen holes and gaps in the metal.

"Wonder how bad it'll be?" Samuel asked, his fingers against the glass.

"I could do with some rain," Gertrude said, removing her scarf and letting Alice out of her pack. The cat hopped into the driver's seat and lay down, cleaning her paws. The old lady put her hands underneath her armpits and frowned at the west.

"I don't like this storm that's coming," she said. "I feel ill. This ain't fun, Samuel. My heart's saying we might go the way of Dorothy and Toto when it hits."

The top layer of ash blew with the wind, but underneath remained still, hardened together as it had cooled over the past week. It made the world look sick, as if the storm had picked a scab off the land, revealing the ugliness underneath. Gertrude wondered how many bodies might have suddenly lost their burial shroud.

With a sudden gust of air, the storm arrived. Lightning struck in constant waves, illuminating the land in a dizzying flash, a hellish strobe light. The thunder hit like a physical force, booming and crashing as if the foundations of heaven were being torn asunder.

"Sweet Jesus!" Gertrude cried, her palms across her eyes.

Samuel watched, fascinated. His eyes ached in the brightness, but he could not look away. White veins pulsed in the clouds. The ash blew not eastward but upward, as if lifted to the heavens by God's command. The car groaned. Its windows cracked. Deep in the distance, he watched a line of trees crack and fall.

Through it all, the world remained dry.

"Please, Jesus, save us!" Gertrude wailed.

As if a monster had suddenly awakened within him, Samuel pulled a pistol from his pocket and struck her atop the head with the butt. Before she even knew she was hurt, Gertrude slumped in her seat, the storm mercifully absent in her dreams.

*

When Gertrude awoke, her ankles were tied together, her hands bound separately behind her. The storm was a rumbling thing in the far distance. Their fire burned anew in its pit, and standing in the red light, gun in hand, was Samuel.

She let out a low moan, every bone in her body aching. The image of Samuel was so terrible she told herself it was a dream. Her eyes closed, but not for long. A rough hand grabbed her face and pulled it upward. She looked and saw Samuel, monster Samuel, his bloodshot eyes wide and wild.

"Do you know why I was travelling east?" he asked her.

"Where's Alice?" she asked, ignoring him.

He struck her. Blood dripped down her lip.

"I asked you a question. You know why I was travelling east? Because I have something now. I have *hope*. Too long our nation rotted under old ideas, worn archaic foundations to an otherwise great society. But we'll have to build anew, don't you understand that, Gertrude?"

"Ms. Henderson," she said, her head lolling side to side as if her neck were rubber. Her body was propped against the side of the car. She missed the protection of her scarf. The storm had awakened the ash, filling the air with its sting. "Impolite brat like you should learn manners."

"Manners?" Samuel laughed. "Billions of people are dying, and you want me to use *manners?* You see what I mean? Everyone's blind. No one sees the big picture, but I do. Remember when I said I had a question to ask you? Well, I'm asking now. You just couldn't keep your little vanity, your 'Sweet Jesus' and your feeble prayers to yourself. So now I'm asking, Ms. Henderson."

He knelt down, the gun rocking in his hand. He looked her in the eye, and she glared back, unafraid.

"Do you believe in God, Gertrude?" he asked.

"Believe in him more than I believe in you," she said. He tilted his head to one side.

"Is that so? Might I ask how? Or more importantly, why?"

"Because he's been so good to me," she said. Samuel laughed before she could continue.

"Good to you? Good! Have you lost your eyes, old hag? Look around you. How many corpses have you passed on your walk east? How many cars filled with families huddled together, sobbing as they fucking died in each other's arms? Hell, even God's precious trees and flowers are nothing but death beneath the ash."

"We walk in the end of days," Gertrude said. "But I wouldn't expect a Sunday school-skipping truant like you to know a thing about that."

Samuel shoved the barrel against her neck. He didn't appear mad. He seemed calm, and that scared her far more than anything else he'd done.

"If God exists, he's a murderer," he said. "My wife, my son, he filled their lungs with ash and tossed me their bodies to bury. So I deny him. He doesn't exist. Those that can look upon this wasteland and say he does are diseased. They're sick. Now I'll ask you again, Gertrude: do you believe in God? You still think he exists?"

She swallowed. The knot on her head from where he'd struck her pounded with rhythmic throbs of pain.

"I do," she said. "And he does."

Samuel reached around her back and untied one of her hands. He crushed her arthritic fingers in his grip, then slammed it against the car. Holding her wrist, he aimed and pulled the trigger. The gun fired, the noise loud and painful. Gertrude screamed as blood erupted from her palm. She tensed and pulled, sobbing as she tried to hold her wounded hand against her chest, but Samuel would not relent.

"Please," she cried. "Just take care of Alice. She's just a dumb cat, ain't done nothing wrong. When I'm, When I..."

Samuel let go of her hand and knelt down. He suddenly spoke with compassion, his voice soft and his smile warm.

"Don't you get it?" he asked her. "God is like your damn cat. Alice doesn't exist, Gertrude. You've spent your days talking to no one."

Samuel paced before the fire while Gertrude bled atop her jacket. Her sobs quickened, and she felt like she might faint. Her hurried breaths gagged as ash pooled on her tongue.

"We can be a stronger nation," Samuel said, talking to the hidden stars. "A better nation, smaller perhaps, but a fit man can defeat a sickly giant. For years the world looked to the U.S. for guidance, but now they look to us with pity. They mock what they have long abandoned."

Gertrude closed her eyes, and slowly her lips mouthed words. When Samuel saw this, he snapped. His fist struck her cheek, rattling her teeth.

"Don't you dare pray for yourself," he snarled at her.

"Not myself," she said, looking at him with her tired, weepy eyes.

Samuel turned cold at that. He aimed the gun at her forehead.

"I'll ask you again," he said.

"I know you will," she replied.

"No one will hear your answer. You won't be a saint. There's no one to impress, no one to convince."

"I'm here."

"Last chance. Don't be a fool, Gertrude. Open your eyes. Like your cat. Like your goddamn cat."

"Ask already."

"Do you believe in God, Gertrude?"

Last Words
by Michael Crane

As Harold waited for his son, he looked out his window and stared at the ash covering the ground. Florida might've been better off than other parts of the country, but the ash was still there. A constant, grim reminder of what had just transpired only a few weeks ago. The sky appeared forever gray and showed no signs of changing whatsoever. It looked like winter in the Midwest.

A damn shame, he thought. Still, he was alive. That was what really mattered. Many had died and lost loved ones. There were parts of the country that wouldn't recover for years to come. A tragic situation, yes, but he was still alive.

He just wished that his son Gary felt the same way.

It wasn't because Gary was acting coldhearted. Quite the opposite. His son was devastated, but the truth was people said horrible things after a nasty breakup. You never meant the things you said in the heat of an argument. He tried to tell him that many times, but Gary seemed to think it was the end of everything as he knew it.

At least he agreed to come over and talk. He was thankful for that much.

He heard a knock at the door. It startled him, but he collected himself and he went to the door with a smile on his face.

"Glad you could make it," he said.

His son only gave him a simple nod. He looked terrible. He hadn't shaved in days. His face was smeared gray with ash. Even though he was wearing a long jacket, Harold noticed that his clothes were terribly wrinkled. He also smelled the scent of booze.

Not the best state to see your own son in, but it could've been worse. Far worse.

He let him inside and told him to make himself comfortable.

"Got any scotch?" Gary asked.

Harold held in his frown. "Um, afraid I don't," he lied. "Please, just have a seat."

Gary rolled his eyes, but did as he was told. He sat on the couch while Harold chose the recliner next to it.

"I can't stay long."

"Fine. Plans?"

"No. Just can't stay long."

Harold was at a loss for words. He didn't even know where or how to begin. The fact that his son didn't want any part of it didn't make things easy, either, but he had to be strong. *Focus*, he thought. He feared for his son's life. Dammit, he had to try something. *Anything*.

"Gary, you know I love you. Right?"

Again, his son rolled his eyes. "Dad, I'm not twelve."

"That don't mean anything. I'm just trying to tell you that I love you… and I'm worried about you, to be honest."

"Worried about what, exactly?" Gary asked, without looking at his father.

How could he possibly explain to his son everything he was feeling without coming off as one of those dreadful TV dads that everybody made fun of? That was his biggest fear. To come off as insincere or rehearsed. If he did, he'd lose him. Gary wouldn't listen to a damn word he had to say. He had to be very careful, while at the same time, make it so he understood the seriousness of the situation.

"I know you haven't been sleeping much," he started. "Since after… you know."

Gary grunted.

"I mean, I know how awful it is," Harold said while leaning forward a little. "And I'm truly sorry that it happened, but you know… you had no control or say over it. You know what I mean?"

Gary rubbed his nose and gave a few snorts. "Yeah, well I doubt I'm the only one not sleeping lately, dad. It ain't just me. A lot of people died."

"Yes, and I understand that. But you and me… we're alive. That has to count for something, right?"

Gary chuckled and shook his head. "Look, I don't know what this is all about. If this is some sort of *I-hope-you-don't-off-yourself* speech, you can save it. All right? I'm fine. Just having a hard time accepting what happened to Janet."

"Yes. I understand. Completely. But you had no part in her death."

Gary leaned forward and put his face in his hands. He gave out an exhausted sigh.

"I don't know," he said into his hands. "I told her moving to California wasn't a good idea." He took his face away from his hands and patted down his legs. "I did. I told her, 'Don't go there. Nothing good will come of it.' I didn't *know*…"

"Nobody did. That's the point. Nobody knew that things were going to turn out like this. That's the way life is, Gary. You can't expect or prepare for everything. You can only act accordingly to whatever is thrown your way."

Gary leaned into the sofa, his eyes watching the ceiling. He blew some air out and scratched his chin. "I was bitter, Dad. I was really fucking bitter when she left me."

Harold didn't normally like it when his son cursed, even if he was thirty. However, he let it go. Just the fact that he was even talking about it was a victory of sorts.

"Son, I think just about everybody gets bitter after a breakup."

"Yeah, but that don't excuse it, you know? I said some awful, *awful* things. And now? I can't take 'em back." He looked at his father. "You have any idea what a terrible feeling that is? Not being able to say you're sorry to somebody? Not being able to call that person up and say, 'Hey, I was an asshole. I was a goddamned sonofabitch, and I'm sorry.'" He paused. "I was real thick-headed. I immediately put blame on her when she called it off between us."

The fact that his son was holding onto so much guilt broke his poor, old heart. What could he possibly say to comfort him? What could anybody say? Here was a man distraught over irrevocable last words. How did you take that weight off someone's shoulders, regardless of whether it belonged there in the first place?

"You're not to blame. Not for that."

Gary got up and began pacing the room.

"See, that's what everybody says to me. Why blame yourself, Gary? You didn't cause it. How do you know? Huh? We never really know the true power of our words until it's too late. If a wife tells her husband that she hopes he dies of a heart-attack and it actually comes to pass, did she cause that? Who's to say?"

"When was this?" Harold asked.

Gary groaned and rubbed his temples. "It *didn't* happen, Dad. I'm trying to make a point here. That's all. I said something awful to Janet. Those were my last words to her. And now, I've got to live with it somehow." He rubbed harder and let out another groan.

"You will get past this, Son. I promise, you will."

A sigh came out of Gary. He looked at his father while he remained standing. "You remember when I was in Third Grade and I nearly choked on some hard candy?"

He nodded. "I believe so."

"I thought I was going to die. Scariest thing in the world when you're that little. Eventually, I coughed it up and was all right, but my whole class freaked out." He paused and licked the corner of his mouth. "I never told you the whole story. What happened was that I did terrible on a test. The teacher passed out candy to those who did well, and one of my friends got one. This kid, Jake. Don't know if you remember him. Not sure I had him over all that much… but that's beside the point. Anyway, when I saw Jake got one, I bugged the hell out of him to let me have it. When he told me no, I threw a goddamned hissy-fit. Finally, he just threw it my way and said, 'Fine.'"

"Okay."

"But you know what he said as I put it in my mouth? And I swear to God, I'll *never* forget this. Under his breath, he said, 'I hope you choke on it.' I swear, Jake said those exact words. I shit you not." He looked towards one of the windows and curled his lips. "He didn't mean it, of course. I know that much… but damn if it didn't happen…"

"People don't have that kind of power. Things don't happen just because you wish it. Good, or bad. That's not the way life works."

Gary looked at his father. "Perhaps, but I don't know. All I know is I was freaked out by it. And Jake? He took it hard. Wouldn't speak to anybody for a week. He was convinced he was to blame. He asked me if it was his fault one day, and you know what? I didn't have an honest answer for him. I didn't know." He looked out the window again.

"It's getting colder, you know. It's freezing out there." He folded his arms and shivered. "So unreal." He shrugged and shook his head. "Whatever. I have to get going." He started walking towards the door.

Harold quickly got up and followed after his son. There was something that didn't fit. Something that Gary was holding onto and hadn't yet revealed.

"Wait."

Gary stopped and faced him.

"You're not telling me the whole story."

"What? The candy episode?" He chuckled. "Look, I'm sorry I wasn't more truthful about that when I was a kid. I was afraid you'd get sore at me for failing a test…"

"No. I'm talking about Janet."

Gary's face grew tight and he gave a nervous cough.

"You told me you were angry at her for leaving you, and that you told her you hated her the last time you two spoke. After she moved to California."

Gary looked down at the floor and was quiet for a moment. A great deal of pain spread across his face, just like a little boy not wanting to admit that he got sent to the principal's office. Harold knew this look very well. It was obvious he had one last thing to say.

"Why would saying that you hated her end her life?" Harold asked. "How would that cause any of this?"

He finally looked at his father in the eyes.

"I didn't tell her I hated her." He rubbed the back of his neck while letting out another sigh. "The last time I spoke to her was a couple of months ago. Just shortly after she moved. I begged her to take me back. Was practically on my goddamn knees. I told her I would do right by her if she gave me another chance."

He chuckled, and the pain in his eyes frightened Harold.

"She wanted no part of it. I exploded and lost my temper. I started shouting."

"What did you say?"

Another pause. "You really want to know?"

"It's important, son."

He was still silent for another moment. He threw his hands into his pockets and kicked at his feet. Without looking at him, he said, "I told her I hoped she died." He looked at his father and nodded. "That's exactly what I said to her. And now, I have to live with that for the rest of my life."

Harold couldn't speak. In that very moment, he wanted to break down in tears. He wanted to say something to his son—hell, maybe even hug him and never let go—but before he could, Gary was out the door.

Refugees
by John Fitch V

Carly Simmons rushed from the Government Center subway station across the red bricked plaza to Boston City Hall. Her black heels clicked as she power-walked, nearly knocking over a tourist staring at a map in his hands.

"Hey, look where you're going!" the tourist barked.

"Sorry," Carly replied. She dug out her BlackBerry and dialed the special number. It rang twice. "Carly here. I'm a few minutes away from meeting with the mayor. What's the status on the ash?"

Carly listened intently before she asked, "Have you seen anything on the satellite pick-up about survivors?" She listened for a few seconds, biting her lip. A pigeon crossed her path. "Alright, so they'll be here soon. I'll call you back after I meet with the mayor."

She hung up and resumed her power walk.

She showed identification at the gate on the northern side of the building. The guards let her in without a second look. Carly thanked them with a smile, even though she had no time for such pleasantries.

The storm approached.

Carly found her way to the mayor's office. She didn't even knock. She walked right in.

The television blared reports from Washington, with a picture-in-picture showing devastation from Denver; the picture was fuzzy, most likely a web-based camera. Every eye in the room stared at the footage, not knowing someone else had joined them until Carly cleared her throat.

"Can I help you?" the receptionist asked after she turned.

"My name is Carly Simmons. I'm an aide to the president. I must speak with the mayor at once."

"He's in a meeting right now –"

"Meeting's over," Carly demanded. The receptionist jumped. "I'll be directing the planning for the coming refugees."

"That's what they're meeting about, though."

"Which way?"

The receptionist pointed through the closed door.

Carly didn't wait for an invitation. She walked past the woman and barged in.

Around a conference table, people argued. Fingers pointed every which way. Maps and blue prints littered the table, along with Styrofoam Dunkin Donuts cups and slivers of strudel.

Carly sought out the only well-known face, that of the mayor. He sat at the end of the table, amid the hubbub surrounding him. He'd clearly given up trying to control his own meeting. He rubbed his temples, as if a headache settled on the sides of his skull.

I came just in time, Carly thought. She walked to the table and slammed her briefcase on it.

Everyone jumped. The mayor groaned a tad.

"I hope I'm not disrupting something important," Carly said. A slight grin crossed her face.

"Who the hell are you?" the mayor said.

"I'm Carly Simmons from Washington. I'm here to direct refugee movements. The rest of you can skedaddle; you'll receive orders soon."

The others began arguing to her – not with her, for Carly disregarded each in turn. She finally whistled, cutting off their bitching and moaning.

"This is officially a federal matter now, boys and girls. The president requests you follow my lead. Homeland Security is aware of what's going on, and they're monitoring the flow of traffic headed east. People are coming, a lot of people, and Boston has to be ready. They'll need places to stay, and no, they can't afford a hotel for the rest of their lives. Now if you'll excuse the mayor and I, we have a lot to discuss."

A lot of grumbling followed the department heads out the door. The last one turned and flipped her off.

Carly simply waggled her fingers up by her face as the door shut.

"Thank God you came when you did," the mayor said. He walked to his desk, took two aspirin, and chased them with water. "Those people were going to be the death of me; or at least my mind. What's the situation?"

"Survivors are coming in droves. Highways are clogged. Intel suggests people will try to get off the highway at the first exit that isn't backed up for miles. That means Sturbridge, Auburn, maybe even Millbury. It's possible to close the exits and corral as many as we can into Boston. The president is on the phone with the governor now, and he's trying to do just that. There's loads of open space here: City Hall Plaza, the Public Gardens, Fenway Park, the Garden. We have to set up tent cities in the open areas and cordon off areas inside the Garden. We want to avoid any Katrina-esque incidents."

"It'll be like 1978 all over again," the mayor muttered, referring to the unexpected February blizzard that stranded fans inside the old Boston Garden during the Beanpot hockey tournament. "What are we going to do about food? How are we going to feed all these people?"

Carly frowned.

"The first few weeks will be a stretch. Meat will go quickly, I suspect. So will other standard essentials."

"That usually happens here; New Englanders hit the grocery store and clean out milk and bread when the weathermen call for snow flurries."

"But this isn't just snow flurries, Mayor D'Angelo. This is a storm of not only people, but ash and rock that will change the fate of this country." Carly paused, as if choked up. She took a deep breath. "As I was saying, the first few weeks will be a stretch, but as soon as we get a full count of how many people survived, we can re-route government-supplied food to the areas that need it most."

"You're talking about a completely new census. That could take months, Miss Simmons. These people will starve within six weeks."

"We're hoping it won't take that long, which means we'll need to recruit people to handle the proper counts. That must be done immediately. We can't let anyone settle in. Those counts are imperative. And until we can figure out which areas need the most food, it's going to be strictly on a rationing system. Grocery stores are going to be shut down for the time being; hopefully not more than a day or two."

"That's not going to work. We'll have riots on your hands if you close the grocery stores. Bostonians are going to go nuts when they find out."

"They'll behave. We won't give them a choice. The government is taking a firm grasp; we're not going to let this disaster get out of hand. We've learned from prior mistakes, and we'll make sure it's peaceable. The president has ordered all divisions of the military on stand-by; the governors will probably follow the directives of the president and ready their respective National Guard units."

D'Angelo sighed.

"Where else did the president send people like you to?"

"Every major city on the eastern seaboard will have a federal liaison."

"They obviously have reservations about what's going to happen."

Carly nodded.

"Mister Mayor, I'm going to be frank with you. We are just as scared about what's going to happen as everyone else. This ash cloud has already killed millions of people, and it's going to kill more. Every farm in the bible belt is gone. Our ecosystem is in ruins. Food is going to be hard to come by; hell, even a packet of Skittles and a cup of coffee will soon be considered a luxury. We're going to have riots over this, that I know, and the president knows that, too. Martial law will rather quickly become the norm on the east coast; what remains of Congress won't like it, especially the Republicans, but he's having his people draft a bill to vacate elections for the time being. We have to calm the people and tell them they won't starve, but –" Carly paused, biting her tongue.

"But what?"

"We're hoping that some people *do* starve, and that the ash cloud buries more cars on the eastbound highways. That way, there will be more food for everyone else."

D'Angelo's eyes widened, his mouth opening and closing, as if trying to find words.

"That's despicable," he sputtered at last.

"It is, but it could be the only way we'll control the food distribution. We were lucky to get government-issued cheese and meat out of Los Angeles, San Francisco and Seattle before the ash cloud fully covered the west coast; those ships are taking a very long way to get around the globe. It may be two or three weeks before they get here, if they get here at all. Who knows what will actually be edible by the time they arrive. We can't trust they'll have safe passage through the Indian Ocean. One of the ships that left Los Angeles may stop in Miami, if the captain chooses to take the Panama Canal. After that…" She let the thought hang perilously in the air.

"Has the president reached out to other countries for aid? What can England or our allies do to help us?"

Carly shrugged.

"I'm not sure, sir. To be honest, it doesn't look good. Our experts think that the rest of the world will hurt by this, too, just not as bad. The world's in for a state of nuclear winter. We haven't released that information to the public yet."

The mayor began pacing. He pinched the bridge of his nose, as if the headache moved to the center of his face.

Carly saw the world on his shoulders, weighing the man down.

"So we have to prevent anarchy from taking a hold of the people, and hope some people starve to death for everything to be all right. That's not exactly how I envisioned this," D'Angelo said.

"I don't think it's actually what anyone had in mind, but we have to hope for the best."

D'Angelo sighed again.

"Alright, Miss Simmons. Let's get down to the nitty gritty."

*

"Rationing? Are you kidding me? I have a family of six to feed!"

Then you should have closed your legs at some point, you dumb bitch, Carly thought with a smile. She stood at the head of a long line of Bostonians in City Hall Plaza, who came out to complain – loudly – about the refugees looking to make the great northeastern city their home.

"Ma'am, we feel this is the best way to handle the crisis we're under. The government is taking control of the situation, and we expect to feed everyone."

"The government is taking control?!" one man protesting, his accent thick and heavy. "They took over our health care, and now they're going to tell us when and how much to eat? Are they going to tell us when we can take a piss, too?"

"Are you fucking stupid?" Carly retorted. The crowd quieted, as if stunned by such a response from a well-dressed public official.

"We need to work together," she said. "We'll all need to make sacrifices, regardless of what we believe in." Sprinkles of gray began falling on the crowd. Many people cried as the ash accumulated lightly. "For all we know, we won't get many refugees here. And besides, the east coast is a very large place; stations like this have been set up along the coast so many cities will see refugees, not just Boston."

The crowd's voice rose again, but Carly lifted her hands in a quest for silence.

"Folks, I know this is difficult for all of you, but please, let's not think about ourselves. We're going to see many tired, cold, hungry and *scared* people coming here. These are people who have lost their homes, relatives, friends, possessions. In short, they've lost everything. You folks still have homes and food in your refrigerators. These people have nothing except the clothes on their backs: We're standing here at the possible end of the United States as we know it, and all you can bitch about is the government rationing out what little food we have? Grow the fuck up and show some consideration for your fellow man."

One by one, the crowd silenced itself. Carly's words pinballed inside their minds, striking a resonant chord.

Carly looked out and saw many ashamed faces staring at the ground.

She choked for a second, then recovered.

"Folks, if you have any clothes you can donate, old clothes that you don't wear any longer, please consider dropping it off at one of our drop-off stations. These people are going to need some things to wear, and if you could help them out, the government would appreciate it." She looked down at her clipboard. "I think that covers it."

Carly gave no closing salutation. She turned and walked away from the podium while the murmurs of the crowd chased after her. She did not look to see if any of the people stayed; she had bigger worries to deal with at the moment.

She pulled out her BlackBerry and dialed the number again.

"What's the situation? Where are the people coming to Boston?" She listened for a second. "The State Police set up traffic boards to direct people to Government Center, so they should be here soon. Thankfully the parking garage at Haymarket is pretty empty. It's going to be a permanent lot now." She looked up as the ash fell like gray snow. "If their cars can make it."

Carly hung up and looked out toward Congress Street.

Soon there would be ash-covered cars with out of state plates lining up along the sidewalks. They'll be wondering about their new home and where they'll stay. With them came a million questions, and so very few answers.

God, I only hope I'm strong enough not to tell these people the truth. There is so little hope – for any of us.

A tank rolled by on Congress, the first of many as the National Guard arrived.

She hoped the situation would not get out of hand.

*

"This isn't going to be like camping out, daddy," Cassie said, her whiny 6-year-old voice coming right to the point. "When we went camping last year, the ground was soft and the air smelled nice. This," -she waved her hand around, indicating the jagged edged bricks that encompassed their new surroundings- "isn't so soft. And that tree smells like pee."

Her father, Daniel, cringed.

"Sweetie, I know it's bad, but we have to keep our spirits up."

Cassie pouted and sat on the granite steps between City Hall and the squat federal building.

Daniel's heart broke; he didn't like his daughter upset.

But what can I do? he thought. *We've been uprooted and cast from our home. It's hard for any little girl to deal with. Hell, it's hard for me to deal with.* He clenched his eyes. *Damn it, Carolyn! Why did you have to take that flight to Denver?*

Daniel wanted to scream. He refused his grief, though: Daniel, now a single parent, had to be strong for his only child. The grief welled.

There were many times during their trip from Columbus to Boston that Daniel wanted to pull over and let the torrent of tears wash over and out of him. It wasn't a smart idea to let the grief build up; his elders back home in Denver had told him that everyone needed to grieve at some point.

Just thinking about their words, now only in his memories, made him want to flee. Their bodies were no doubt under several feet of ash.

It's not fair, Daniel thought as he sat down next to his daughter. *It's not fair that Cassie and I live while the rest of our family perishes.* A solo teardrop did a long, slow march down his cheek. He wiped it away before Cassie could see it.

A tissue appeared out of thin air next to him. The sight startled him, but when his tear-filled eyes adjusted, he saw who held the tissue.

His jaw fell.

"I thought you might need this," the woman said.

Daniel took it without a word, until his manners caught up with him.

"Thank you."

My God, she is beautiful, he thought. *She almost looks like my Carolyn.*

"My name is Angela, and I'm with the city of Boston. I'm just taking a count of the refugees."

"What do you need from us?" he asked. "It's really just my daughter and I... now."

He kept his tears at bay.

Angela marked her clipboard. Daniel could see a stack of papers held down upon it. He also saw no ring on her finger.

"And what are your names, and where are you from?"

"I'm Daniel Drake, and this is my daughter, Cassie. We're from Columbus."

"O-H."

"I-O," Daniel replied instinctively with a smile. Cassie leaned on his side. He wrapped his daughter up in a small blanket. A man in fatigues with a semi-automatic rifle walked by, looking around at everyone. Daniel eyed him warily.

"What's going on? Why is G.I. Joe acting like he's looking for Destro?"

Angela shrugged.

"I don't really know, sir. I haven't been told much, but —"

A scream tore the air near the pavilion stage. Feet pounded the bricks in a rush, refugees swarming volunteers.

"It's food!" someone yelled.

"Hey, let's keep order here!" the military man said, pushing his way through the crowd. Someone grabbed the gun and downed him, issuing the butt of the rifle into the man's gut. More people surged forward. Other men with rifles tried to fight their way through the horde, but it was useless.

Daniel and Angela watched from the top level. They sat there horror stricken, as if the people below had lost their minds.

Daniel looked to the crowd, then down to Cassie, who had fallen asleep despite the tumult. He looked back to the mob below, which now saw more military men trying to control them.

It wasn't working, Daniel could see. Loaves of bread took off like planes departing Logan, coming down as if clueless pilots were at the controls. Rounded cheese flew up and landed without bouncing.

Then the gunshots cracked. Screams blistered the air, caroming off the concrete and bricks. Cassie woke from the noise, afraid. Daniel picked her up, the blanket clinging to her. He moved toward Congress Street. Angela, however, stayed rooted to the spot, unmoving, watching the chaos unfold like a terrible dream.

Daniel ran for the stairway near the federal building. Several others ran alongside. He made the quick dash carrying his sweet burden as fast as he could. He hurried north along Congress Street and looked for his car.

He found his car covered in a light coating of ash. He wiped the handle and opened the door.

"Get in the back seat, sweetie," he said.

"Daddy, where are we going? Another car ride? I thought we were staying here."

"I know honey, but just do as I ask, okay?"

Cassie didn't put up another argument. She got in and buckled her seat belt by herself before Daniel hurried around the front to his seat.

A mob spilled out of City Hall Plaza. Several carried bricks, as if they ripped them out of the ground. They walked north.

Daniel tried the ignition. The engine groaned, but it wouldn't start.

"Come on, turn over you stupid, fucking –"

"Language, daddy!"

"Sorry, sweetie. Sometimes I need to –"

Glass shattered around them. Cassie screamed as the brick zipped through the windshield. Daniel gasped. The car began rocking as the throng reached them. More glass shattered, this time on other cars.

"Shit!" Daniel tried the engine again, and finally it sang a revving chorus. Daniel laughed.

"Gun it, daddy! I'm scared!"

Daniel didn't care there were people surrounding his car, or that there was a large hole in the middle of his windshield. He put the car in drive and drove his right foot onto the accelerator, turning the wheel left. He didn't hit the brake.

Several of the rioters fell to the ground, grasping their broken legs and hips. Some landed on the hood of Daniel's Mazda, but couldn't hang on for long as he sped away from the scene. They cracked their heads on the pavement. Most got out of the way. Some weren't so lucky.

Daniel made a U-turn when he got to Faneuil Hall, heading north on Congress. He thanked God for the steel fencing on the traffic island. He sped away toward the North End, his dented Mazda keeping to the road. Ash slid off the car like snow on the highway in winter.

A tank cut him off as he meandered closer to the submerged Central Artery. Daniel swerved and nearly hit the stationary military men, all of whom lifted their weapons after the fact.

Cassie just cried.

Bullets tinkled against the chassis. None hit the tires.

Sweat slicked Daniel's forehead as he drove away, beads sliding down his bloodless face.

"We need to find a safe place, sweetie."

"Where?"

"I don't know. Let's just drive and hope we don't find any road closures."

They didn't find any as they drove north out of Boston; but they didn't stop anywhere in Massachusetts. They looked northward to less populated areas – places where they would be the only refugees, places where they could grieve privately.

Daniel also wanted to change their names. For what he just did on the streets of Boston, he didn't want to be found by anyone.

Not even by Angela.

A Harmless American
by David Dalglish

Javier watched her swim until she drowned.

The Rio Grande glowed majestic in the pale light of the moon. He was far from the floodlights, the big camps and the bridges. The water flowed quiet and wide, every inch of its surface covered with ash. The far side was a vast stretch of dry packed earth, whatever grass there long dead from the darkened sky. Because of how open and bare the approach, and how far they were from any nearby roads and bridges, Javier had only a spotlight the size of his fists to aim and search the waters. He hadn't seen her, though, only heard her last desperate cry.

"Help!" she cried, and even though he spoke no English, Javier knew that universal beg. It'd only been shouted across the river a million times over the past few months. He grabbed the light, which sat on an emptied crate beside him. After a minute, he found her, a young teenage girl struggling against the current. She was halfway across, but no longer swimming. Just thrashing, flailing, fighting a losing battle. Her gasps were uneven, and every bit she drank was poison.

Javier shook his head and pulled his coat tighter about him. They always underestimated how cold the Rio Grande could be. Even in Mexico the sun was a rare thing, its warmth fleeting. Rolling down from the mountains, it was an iceflow coated with ash, and at its bottom were a thousand corpses.

When the light shone in the girl's eyes, she stopped for a moment. It was always the same, and no matter how many nights he stayed stationed at the border, he never thought he'd get used to it. A look would flash briefly across the swimmer's face, their tired, scared eyes filling with both fear and desperate hope. Then it'd slowly fade as they realized there would be no help, no swimmers, no ropes or liferafts. Just the dreadful noise of the waters as they swam on, fighting cold, ash, current, and darkness.

And then if they did survive, well…

Javier drew his pistol, checked the clip, and then rest it on his hip. In the end, there was no need. The girl's thrashing slowed, and her screams for help slowly faded. The river took her, pulled her facedown southward. Javier shook his head, feeling a chill work its way up his spine.

Too cold, he thought. *Too damn cold.*

He smoked to pass the time, not caring that the soft orange glow of the tip might hurt his night vision. The way he saw it, the less he saw, the better. Nothing could compare to those first hellish nights after the Caldera had erupted. If the moon was covered and the stars dimmed, sometimes he'd imagine arms sticking up in the water, heads bobbing just above the surface, and the wail of the wind would seem to carry the voices of the drowning…

A thump, just to his left. He stood, knocking over the spotlight with his elbow. Swearing, he pulled a flashlight out from his pocket and flicked it on. With his other hand he grabbed his gun from the ground and then he began searching. It didn't take long to find her. A thick log had washed up against the shore, and clinging to it was a young girl. She looked four, maybe five. It was hard to tell with such poor light, the ash clinging to her like dark snow. She was crying, sobbing a word in English over and over again. When the light of his flashlight shone in her eyes, she squinted and looked up at him.

The gun was heavy in his hand. The girl stared, just stared. Her eyes were green. Her nose was small, her ears almost like those of an elf. Crying. So small, and crying.

"We feed our own," he said to her, as if she'd understand. He moved his finger to the trigger, remembering what he'd been trained. Never place your finger on the trigger unless you were ready to fire. Staring down at her, he wondered if he truly was ready. He aimed the gun. The girl was old enough to recognize what it was, but she only closed her eyes and clutched the log. Her feet swayed in the waters. Her skin was so pale, and her lips quivered from the cold. Or maybe it was fear.

His finger slipped off the trigger.

"Come here," he said, offering his hand. The girl took it, and with a quick tug, he dragged her out and brought her to his station. He had a small tent, a chair facing the water, and his crate. Within the tent was a small cooler filled with clean water. He wrapped her in the blankets to his bed and then gave her a bottle to drink.

"Name?" he asked her in spanish. She stared and shivered. "Your name?"

"Leann," the girl said, her eyes suddenly lighting up as she realized what he wanted. She rattled over a bit more of English, but Javier held a finger to his lips. She nodded and stayed quiet.

Javier looked about, feeling panic claw at his gut. He'd helped a survivor. On his watch, someone had made it across. It didn't matter her age, or how little food she'd eat and water she'd drink. If someone found out, he was in deep shit. What to do? What could he do? Perhaps he could find her a safehouse back at town, but even leaving his post could get him disciplined, if not shot. Deserters, even momentary ones, had become the equivalent of war criminals in the eyes of the Mexican people.

Light flashed over the outside of his tent, faint and distant. Javier swore, his eyes scouring the tent.

"Bed," he said, pointing. Leann climbed atop, seeing his fear. He shook his head and pointed underneath.

"Hurry," he told her, not caring if she understood or not. His bed was a simple cot, the space underneath it narrow, but she was a small girl, with a hint of starvation on her bones. Hoping she could hide herself appropriately, he bolted out of the tent and made for his chair.

"Javier?" called a voice. He felt his gut tightened. He knew who approached, and it was the last person he wanted to see at that moment.

"Yeah, Sergio?" he asked as he sat. His heart thudded as Sergio neared, walking along the edge of the river. He realized the spotlight still lay on the ground. He was just bending over to get it when a hand touched his, also reaching for the light.

"Holy hell," Javier said, jerking his hand back. Up came the spotlight, spinning around, and then resting on the crate. Sergio stared at him, an eyebrow raised.

"Something wrong?" he asked.

Sergio was a skinny man, dark-complexion, his hair thick and black. From their many talks, Javier knew he was intelligent, cold, and dedicated to his post at the border with belief bordering on fanaticism. The river was his church, a gun his bible, and he baptized the dead in its waters with a frightening intensity.

"Just startled me is all," Javier said, trying to keep his voice sounding bored.

"What happened to your light?" Sergio asked as he picked it up and then sat down atop the crate, the light resting in his lap. He shone it across the Rio, looking, watching.

"Bumped it with my elbow," he said.

Sergio nodded. He reached into his pocket and pulled out a cigarette.

"Something is probably wrong with me," he said as he pulled out his lighter. "Half the world's choking with ash, and here I am blowing more into the wind. Shame that

Yellowstone wasn't full of nicotine. We'd have people running toward it instead of our beloved land, climbing their own fences just to get our death sentence."

He inhaled, the tip flaring orange in the night. Javier scratched at his neck, using it as an excuse to turn toward the tent. It was too dark inside. He couldn't see the bed.

The silence stretched for awhile as Sergio enjoyed his cigarette.

"Real quiet lately," Javier said, trying to make conversation.

"Almost makes me sad," Sergio said. "Were you here at the beginning?"

"Acuña," Javier said. "I was at the bridge."

Sergio chuckled.

"*Rayos*, you've seen worse than I. What was it like?"

Javier reached over and grabbed a cigarette from Sergio's pack, then held it out while he waited for the lighter. Memories floated before his eyes as the tiny flame sparked. Thousands of people charging the barricades, some with firearms, but most with nothing but clothes, suitcases, and their young ones. Gunned down, all of them, yet still they'd rushed ahead, as if driven on by a greater terror than bullets could bestow. Finally one of the generals had given a last, desperate order. Cars and civilians still flooding across it, they'd blown the bridge to hell and watched it topple.

"I don't want to talk about it," Javier said as the cigarette finally lit.

"I was down by Matamoros." His eyes seemed to twinkle in the light of the cigarette. "The water's thin there. Hardly any makes it to the ocean. Once heard some gringo say that any drop that makes it to the great blue is wasted. Makes you wonder if god unleashed Yellowstone on them all to teach them a lesson, one gigantic lesson written in ash on the U.S. chalkboard. What we do to the earth don't mean shit compared to what it can do right back to us."

He shifted positions, trying to get comfortable atop the crate. The light went from resting on his right leg to his left.

"Anyway, being so shallow and the land so flat, this meant people thought they could swim across. We barricaded the bridge with so much barbed wire and sandbags, most decided they'd try their luck with the water. So our commander, real tough ass named Miguel, he starts lining us up along the edge, just like a firing squad. That's what we were, too. We waited until they were close, and I mean close. You could see the fear in their eyes, smell the mud on their clothes. And then we fired. And fired. Almost thought I'd run out of clips, and I was taking my time, too, not being wasteful like the others around me."

"Sounds like it was awful," Javier said.

Sergio shone the light at his face, and when he winced at the brightness, he plunged back into darkness. The light shone past him, toward his tent, then back to the water.

"You look pretty pale," Sergio said. "You need something to drink?"

"I'm good," Javier said.

Sergio shrugged.

"You're not even close, by the way. Awful doesn't begin to describe it. They were *walking* across the river by the end. The bridge of the dead, some wiseass near me named it. Name stuck, too, until later that night we destroyed it with dynamite. Just like Acuña's bridge, we had to topple it to protect our families."

"You ever think what it'd be like to be on the other side?" Javier asked as the wind picked up, cold and full of dust. "Try to think what it'd be like to be so scared you'd rush headfirst into gunfire? To be so scared you'd walk across the dead, all while guns are firing and people are dying?"

His cigarette dwindling, Sergio tossed it into the river and reached for another.

"You can't think like that," he said. "You ever think how much food they'd eat when they got here? How much water they'd drink? For every one we shoot across the river, ten die of starvation back in Mexico City. You can't think of them as harmless. They're victims of nature, not us. Hell, blame god if you want. He let the fucker erupt in the first place."

"Yeah, but sometimes, the women, their children…"

Sergio snapped his lighter shut and sucked on his cigarette.

"They all eat. Rationing only goes so far. And no matter what we did, our own would sneak them food. The weak-hearted will give them water, share their scraps. It's like too many don't see the winter coming, see starvation waiting like a lion to devour us all. You know what people will do when they're hungry? They'll kill one another. Father's will butcher their neighbor to feed their own kids. Mothers will smother babies to end their suffering. We'll become a warzone, a country of graves."

He shifted the floodlight back to his other leg.

"Even scared, wet little girls will steal if they're hungry. There's no such thing as a harmless American, not here, not now. They're no longer from the land of the free and the brave. They're from the land of ash, and its citizens are dead, all dead. They just don't know it yet."

Javier stood and used his fists to pop his back. As he sat back down, he shifted his hip and let his hand rest on the hilt of his gun.

"Sure you don't need a drink?" Sergio asked, nodding toward the tent. Javier shook his head. Sergio shrugged. "Suit yourself."

He resumed searching the waters with his floodlight. Every now and then a corpse would float along from further upriver, and his light would linger, waiting, making sure there was no movement.

"Got to be careful of the floaters," he said.

"I've been at this as long as you," Javier said.

"Never can be too careful, though. You hear about David?"

Javier's fist tightened, unclipping the gun from his holster.

"No," he lied.

"It's a shame," Sergio said, discarding the second cigarette. "He helped a boy cross the river when he thought no one was watching. Turns out he was a relative of some sort, didn't hear what exactly. Nephew, maybe, all the way from Chicago. Not sure I buy that, but whatever. They executed them both two days ago, right in the middle of the town. Didn't even waste a bullet. They used a rope, a *maldito* rope."

Javier held in his shudder.

"Real shame," he said, his eyes locked on the river, fighting an impulse to glance over at his tent.

"What we have to do. What we *all* have to do. I keep hearing whispers, how the winds may shift and bring all those clouds our way. We've been lucky for now, but it could change. Any day they could come, and we have to be ready. We have to be strong."

He stood, setting the light back down atop the crate. His right hand rest atop the hilt of his gun.

"I'm thirsty," he said. "Mind if I steal one of your waters?"

"I'm all out," Javier said, staring up at Sergio. The man turned, and their eyes locked.

"You sure? Maybe I should go look, see if something turns up hiding."

"It'd be a bad idea," said Javier.

"It was from the start."

They both drew, but only one gun fired. Javier was the faster. In the light of his muzzle, he watched Sergio stagger back, a bloody hole in his chest. His knees locked, and then he fell, just another body floating along the Rio Grande.

Secret Mission
by David Dalglish

"Okay, now open your eyes," Derek's mom said as she finished tucking the package into the waistband of his jeans and hiding it with his shirt.

Derek did. His mom sat on a small cot, her tangled hair hanging before her face, like dark seaweed. Her brown eyes were still beautiful, but Derek always thought his mom was beautiful. Her told her so whenever he got that uneasy feeling that something was wrong, or his mom's smile was too slow in appearing at his antics.

"Don't look," his mom said when he reached for the bottom of his shirt. "This is a secret mission, Derek. You can't let anyone see what is inside the package. You understand?"

"Like the Super-Kid Spies," he said, and her smile made him feel so much better.

"Just like them," she said. "Now find somewhere quiet. Somewhere hidden. Once you're alone, take out the package."

"What do I do with it?"

His mom lay down on the cot, her hands her only pillow.

"You'll know," she said. "Now go. Hurry."

Feeling the importance of the mission swelling his head, he stood tall and looked about the stadium. They slept on the five of the five-yard-line (for how old you are, his mom had said as they spread out her cot). None of the green or painted lines were visible now, not with the thousands of people crammed into them, smothering the turf with pillows, blankets, cots, and bodies. Lots of bodies, everywhere bodies. He smelled them, saw them. Obstacles to his mission.

Knowing the field would be hopeless, he started winding his way toward the opposite end. Lined up like cheerleaders in the endzone were rows of port-o-potties. Derek had to watch his step, though. There was no order to the cots, no reason to the arrangements of the sleeping. He tiptoed past a mother holding two crying babies, both thin as paper dolls. He stepped over a boy a little older than him, careful not to wake him. The older children had grown steadily meaner as the months wore on. None ever wanted to play. All they grumbled about was food.

The noise lessened as he neared the potties, but it never stopped. Even at night the stadium bore a hum, like the sound of a big power generator running on human coughs, screams, tears, and whispers. But other than the people lined up to use the potties, no one slept in front of them, not that he could see. Feeling the package crinkling against his skin, he skipped about the line, careful to show that he wasn't actually needing to go so no one yelled at him.

The smell worsened with every step. The potties were a faded green, sort of like the turf. A few tilted at strange angles, but most were straight and side by side. Flies swarmed above like a cloud. Derek looped around to the back, to where he hoped to find his privacy.

"Pee yew," he said, grabbing his nose. The smell was worse back there, the air stagnant and rancid. He tried breathing through his mouth, but that didn't help. He felt the foulness on his tongue.

Still, he had his mission. What secret agent would let a bad smell defeat him? As he walked behind the port-o-potties, he tried to remember if James Bond ever dealt with something like that.

He didn't get far before he saw the first body, that of an elderly woman. She lay flat on her stomach, her eyes open, her mouth hanging ajar. Her false teeth had come loose and lay crooked on her tongue. Flies swarmed around her like an insect halo. Derek crossed his arms and took a step back. The lady wasn't the first body he'd seen. Over the months, as people got angrier and skinnier, they'd become a common sight.

"There's nothing to eat," his mom had told him when he'd pointed and asked why one sickly looking man had stopped moving, and didn't move even when the men in yellow uniforms came to carry him away. "Nothing left, not even to share."

He'd always seen them afar, and always with people around, covering them with blankets or keeping others away. But there was no one here, so he openly stared. A worm crawled around in his gut, a creeping feeling of unease. The lady's hair was white and muddied. Her fingers were curled, as if she'd died clawing for her life. Her dress had flowers on it.

Derek touched the package in his waistband. The way it crackled he thought it plastic, but it was also soft. He wondered what secret message or gift hid wrapped within. Glancing around, he knew he was alone. The nearest people were up in the rows of bleachers behind the endzone. A few were watching him, but they were far enough away, so he squatted down, putting his back to the dead lady. Something about her made him uneasy.

Just as he was about to pull up his shirt, a hand touched him. He screamed, certain the lady had woken, her curled fingers clutching his bony shoulder as her drooling mouth opened wider, determined to suck out the life that was not rightfully hers. But instead it was a policeman, tired and unshaven.

"Move, kid," he said. His voice brooked no argument. His hand was on his nightstick, and that scared Derek even worse than his voice. He got up and ran, not caring where he was going. His heart thumped in his chest, but a glance back showed the officer was not following, so he slowed. Already he felt lightheaded and out of breath. His stomach grumbled angrily.

His run took him to the tunnels leading to the locker rooms. He'd tried to explore them several times, but too many doors were locked. He had, however, managed to snag a football from a cart, but two older boys had stolen that from him a week later. Men and women sat along the sides of the walls in their respective lines. Some held towels or changes of clothes while others waited empty-handed, their clothes faded and dirty. Derek felt their dead eyes watching him, as if just waiting for him to try to cut in line.

"Back there," one man said, his face covered with a scraggly beard.

"Not showering," Derek said, running back toward the field, then cutting to the right to walk along the wall before the bleachers.

Getting an idea, he found the steps up and then began the climb. He took them one at a time, counting for a little while until he got past thirty. Twin girls ran down the steps, jostling him into a sleeping mom with a very quiet baby in her arms.

"Watch it," the woman said as she stirred and glared. Feeling her hating eyes burning his back, Derek hurried upward. His optimism faded with his energy as he neared the top. He'd hoped to find a corner somewhere, but there were people even there. They slept in the seats, some even stretched out along the aisles atop blankets. He passed a bucket buzzing with flies. Inside reeked. They were using it as a potty, Derek realized. Evidently they were too weak to keep climbing up and down the stairs.

Derek walked along the top, his arms crossed over his chest. His stomach hurt, and had since about halfway through his climb. The people he passed gave him curious glances, those who bothered to look at all.

"Are you lost?" one lady asked. She wore a dark suit and a silver necklace.

Derek shook his head.

"My mom's down there," he said, pointing to the field.

"Ah," the lady said, laying her head back down against the chair. Her smile was a soft comfort. "Good. That's good."

Further along the top he found a large section added atop the stadium. It had once been private, but its windows were smashed. Inside was a broken mess. Derek poked his head in but quickly hurried away. Big men were in there amid the wreckage, and they had a woman with them. She was crying, but not very loud.

Feeling dejected, Derek started back down the steps. His skin itched from where the package pressed against it, slick with sweat.

I have to find somewhere to be alone, he thought. *Mommy will be upset if I don't.*

A big kid shoved him into the railing as he passed by up the stairs, but Derek bit his tongue to hold in his cry. Crying seemed to make them madder.

Somewhere secret. Somewhere alone. Where could he find a place like that? Standing at a railing running perpendicular to the stairs, he looked out across the stadium. Everywhere he saw people. They walked, they talked, they lay on beds and sat in chairs. The whole stadium felt like a swarming mass of people, and it stank of their sweat, fear, and exhaustion. Why would mom give him such an impossible task?

No, he thought, shaking his head. Super-Spies got impossible missions all the time. He wouldn't wimp out. He wouldn't start crying. He wouldn't!

A bit of a spring in his step, he hurried back down to the field, an idea forming. He was small, just a little thing compared to the others. He could hide where the adults could not, not even the big kids. As he weaved his way back to the field, he passed one of the concession stands. For awhile they had been little kitchens, and his mom had taken him there for food, but not anymore. The food was gone. The stand's bars were lowered, its lights off. Trucks had come the first few months with bread and soup, but no longer.

When he reached the field, he started looking for the tractor. They were up in the far northeast, and he'd seen it a couple times, one day climbing up and down it until some adults had yelled at him. He didn't think anyone would yell at him now.

He found it parked to the side of one endzone. Thrilled, Derek let out a whoop. It was big and boxy, less of a tractor and more of an oversized riding mower. Attached to the back was a stretcher, long and flat. It wasn't very high off the ground, but it was enough. Hoping the secret package wouldn't get damaged, he crawled underneath on his belly. He bumped his head twice along the bottom, but he his cry came out as a long hiss. He wouldn't reveal his presence, not now. It was cramped, and he could hardly move, but there was no way anyone else would get to him there in the center.

Excitement tugging at his heart, he untucked his shirt and pulled out the package.

It was indeed wrapped in plastic, though the top was cardboard. Inside was a glob of gummy-worms, fused together from the heat. Derek's mouth watered at the sight. He tore off the top and tossed it aside. Hungry as he was, he carefully separated each worm, tearing at the sides where they had melted together. When he put the first into his mouth and bit down, the sugar spreading across his tongue, he finally did cry.

When his crying stopped, he ate another, and another. Each bite was full of memories of his father sitting to his right in the theater as they watched a movie. He'd always gotten gummies, his father, popcorn. His stomach twisted and coiled, as if angry at the lack of substance as he wolfed down the candy. He didn't care. Snot dripped from his nose, but he wiped his face on his shoulder. He wondered if he'd ever watch cartoons again. If he'd ever return to school and play tag with Mike and Jeffy. If he'd ever see his daddy again.

At last he crawled out from the cart, his fists clenched tight, his face muddy and covered with bits of green turf. He worked his way back to his mom, to her little cot and his superman blankets. When he arrived, she lay very still.

"Mom," he said, touching her shoulder. She didn't move.

"Mom?"

Her eyes flicked open.

"Yes, babe?" she asked.

He held out his hand, two gummy-worms smooshed in his palm. Seeing this, she smiled.

"Thank you," she said, taking them. She didn't chew them, only slowly working them across her tongue as she sucked in the sugar and flavor. Derek joined her on the cart and moved her arm around him as they cuddled, his mom softly crying, his secret mission a wonderful success.

The One That Matters
by Robert J. Duperre

Ash covered the landscape like cold, dead snow. Small lumps scattered throughout the yard, buried in the piles of blowing dust. They might have been objects forgotten during the rush to beat the easterly wind, or perhaps the remains of the chickens the useless feed in the buckets used to nourish. A cold wind blew, revealing a blackened joint. It might have been the elbow or knee of some poor soul who'd come in search of help; help they obviously no longer needed.

Guido grunted and turned away. Nothing he hadn't seen before. He continued around the old farmhouse, back creaking, lungs wheezing. Placing a hand on the back porch's stoop, he rested a moment. His eyes looked skyward. Dark clouds still loomed ominous overhead. They billowed so deep and low they seemed to stretch for miles into the atmosphere. Water fell on the shield of his gas mask. He whisked the drops away with a wipe of his gloved hand, leaving trails of black soot. Another gust of wind caught him unaware, and he shivered at its biting cold.

Turning back to the task at hand, Guido circled his house until he found what he was looking for – a thick, curved metal construction that jutted from the foundation. He dipped beneath its lip, knelt in the mounds of wet, gray powder, and took a large brush from his belt. Originally used to clean the horses' hides, it had gained a new purpose, much like everything else since the Event. He swept the bristles side to side against the grate beneath the steel casing, clearing ash from the gaps in the filter. It was tough work, and his back ached with each stroke, but

Guido Malfi was nothing if not a diligent man. Before long, he'd cleared the filter as best he was able. In another three days he'd have to come out again, but that was still three days he could spend inside, warmed under the cover of many blankets. Three days that he could spend with Her.

*

Guido slid the lock through its catch after he closed the bunker's overhead door. The sound of metal scratching against metal echoed through the small entryway, like fingernails over a chalkboard. He winced, waiting for the reverberations to cease. When they did, he moved to the second door and slid it open.

She was waiting for him. She sat on the couch, still wearing the Bratz pajamas she'd had on when she first arrived. Her brown hair was clumped and ratty, but to him, in the dim yellow light, it looked silky and beautiful. Her eyes lifted. She recoiled for a split second and then smiled. Her teeth were crooked, in bad need of braces she would never get.

He slid the gas mask from his head and took a deep breath. His lungs rattled, but that was okay. He'd lived with worse than that before.

The room was small, barely ten feet by ten, entombed by concrete walls four feet deep. This was Guido's pride and joy – a bomb shelter he'd constructed over the last twenty years, a bomb shelter folks assured him he'd never need. He chuckled. So much for them.

He'd stocked the cubby beneath the shelter with enough canned goods and water to last two years, though the girl had thrown off his initial estimations. Grabbing a flashlight, he lifted the hatch and looked inside. The gas generator that powered the lights and the air filter chugged along below the earth, its exhaust piped out to the surrounding woods. He smiled upon hearing its guttural purr. Snatching a couple cans of peaches from a shelf, he shut the hatchway and turned.

"Do you want some food, Alyssa?" he asked.

The little girl nodded.

"Yes please, Mr. Malfi," she replied.

They sat down to eat.

*

"Tell me one of your stories," said Alyssa. She picked up a syrupy peach with her bare hand and plunked it in her mouth.

Guido stroked his white beard. "Hm. Let's see. I told you about the Kennedy assassination, right?"

She nodded.

"How about G.W. and his plan to dominate the world economy by crashing planes into a couple buildings?"

Again, she nodded.

"How about the moon? Have I talked about that?"

"No," she said with a shake of the head. "Tell me that one."

"Okay. Well, it happened a long time ago, when I was a young'n in college. We and the Ruskies were always at each other's throats, trying to beat each other at everything, as if that would help distract us from knowing one side or the other would soon lose patience and launch the first nuke. One of the meanest competitions was this 'race to space' thing. Whoever landed on the moon would get some sort of bragging rights, take first place in this pissing contest we had going. So one day, we did it. We landed on the moon. The whole world stood up and cheered for us, as if we'd accomplished something. But here's the thing, Alyssa. We never did reach the moon. It was all a ruse. You know what a film studio is?"

She listened intently as he spoke, her chin resting on her fists. She stared at him with those wide eyes of hers, and beneath his stories he felt his heart melting. This little girl was everything to him, and had been since the day she came running into his yard screaming while sirens blared in the background. The announcement had just come over the airways, and everyone was in a panic. Vandals tore through every corner of Mercy Hills, Connecticut, his hometown. The little girl had looked so scared, so on edge, as she arrived at the doorstep of his farmhouse while he was outside sealing the shelter from the rain of ash soon to come. At first, he thought to ignore her, to turn her away like he had the Letts family when they came calling. He hesitated, though, and when he looked in those large, innocent eyes, he remembered the dreams of his youth, the love of his family. The family she'd most certainly lost in the chaos of a crumbling society.

So he'd brought her in. He'd saved her, and that memory filled him with pride. *Daughter*, he thought. *She is my daughter now. Or granddaughter, at least.*

When he finished his story, he smiled. They said their goodnights, climbed into their cots on either side of the room, turned off the lights, and fell asleep.

*

A sound awoke him. It was like static, or baseball cards fastened to the spokes of a bicycle. He sat up, his tired muscles aching, and searched for the pull chord in the dark. He found it dangling above him and yanked. The overhead light clicked on. It took a few moments for his eyes to adjust.

Alyssa was already awake. She sat on her cot, knees pulled to her chest. Her eyes, always wide, were even more so now. The poor girl looked petrified. The strange crackling sounded again.

"What is that?" he asked.

Alyssa pulled her knees closer and buried her head between them.

Guido swung his legs over the side of the cot. The concrete floor was cold beneath his bare feet. The thought came to mind that there might be people outside, desperate people who would do anything, kill anybody, for a chance at survival. He grabbed his baseball bat from above his reading desk and went to the reinforced door. Pressing his ear to it, he listened. There was nothing at first, and then that fizz came again. Only it wasn't coming from beyond the door, he realized. It came from inside the shelter.

He glanced at his desk, walked to it, and sat down. Positioned on the side was his ancient radio, still plugged in. His fingers touched the volume and turned it up. At first there was nothing, and then it crackled. It sounded like static, but beneath, he swore he could hear a voice. He twisted the tuning knob – Guido Melfi believed in the solid construction of the old, and this radio hadn't failed him since his teen years – and slowly, the speaker on the other end broke into startling clarity.

"This is a message for all survivors," the voice said. It was male, polite, and had a thick accent. "My name is Colonel Martin Doucette. Citizens of the United States, we have arrived. We apologize for the delay, but we're here now, and we're here to help. As of this moment, our ships are docked and waiting for your arrival. You will be granted amnesty in France, if you choose to exit your homelands. We will remain docked for a period of one month, and hand out supplies to those that remain behind. The list of safe ports is as follows: Boston Harbor, Groton Harbor, New York Harbor…"

Guido clicked off the radio. One hundred and twelve days of silence after the eruption, and it was the French, the goddamn *French*, who came to their aid. He couldn't help but smile.

They've always gotten a bad rap, he thought. *They may be a bit testy, but hey, they're French, so who could blame them?*

Americans seemed to have forgotten that if it weren't for them, we wouldn't have a country to call home in the first place...

He wheeled around, snapped the radio off, and rushed to the aluminum chest that passed for a closet. Throwing it open, he tore through its contents. Clothes flew this way and that.

"What's going on?" asked Alyssa.

He turned, smiled, and started tossing articles of clothing at her. "These won't fit, but we'll make them," he said.

"We're leaving?" Her face brightened, almost wistful. He'd never seen her like this before, and it was the most gorgeous expression he'd ever laid eyes on. It was as if the months of isolation had stripped away, revealing her as she truly was for the first time.

"Yes, Alyssa," he replied, his heart soaring. "It seems the cavalry finally arrived."

*

The cold outside was intense, the worst it'd been in weeks. Guido did his best to ignore it as he led them down the first of many miles toward the harbor. Alyssa trudged beside him through the wet, mulched ash as they turned down what had once been Main Street. He didn't know what time it was, other than a vague sense of daylight. The dark clouds above, the ones that seemed to rush across the sky yet never get anywhere, were thick as ever. It cast an eerie gloom on the world. For a moment, Guido regretted their decision to leave. *We were safe in the shelter*, he thought. *Nothing could touch us there.* All he had to do was look down at his miniscule travel companion, see the expectant look in her eyes beneath her mask's Plexiglas, and those doubts faded.

Before long they reached the center of town. Most of the houses they passed had crumpled beneath the crushing weight of the ash. Windows were broken, leaf-barren trees

felled, and cars overturned. Thankfully the ash covered all
of these, hiding their atrocities, blanketing them into pale,
gray lumps. That was okay by him.

The road signs were long gone, but that didn't matter.
Guido knew where he was going. It was only three miles to
the highway. From there, a straight shot on 95 until they hit
the connectors that led to Groton. On foot, it might take a
few days, but he'd packed plenty of food in the sled he
pulled behind him. They could camp out at night, or at
least whenever it grew too dark to see. They just had to
make sure not to breathe too deeply with their masks off.

They were almost out of the town boundary when
they heard a loud whooping sound. Shadows darted in
front of him, crossing from one wrecked house to another.
More whoops. A rock skittered across the muck-covered
pavement in front of them, scattering ash to the wind.
Guido placed a hand on Alyssa's shoulder and pulled her in
close.

Figures emerged from the shadows, five of them,
hunched and swaying. They circled like a pack of wolves.
Every once in a while one would screech, and he would
feel Alyssa shiver against his leg.

The figures drew closer, and even in the bleak light he
knew they were male, and young. They wore blood-
drenched scarves over their faces, the color shocking
against the stained gray of their skin. Their eyes danced
with madness as they wielded planks of wood with nails
driven through them. Guido held Alyssa tight and reached
into the cart behind him. He pulled out his trusty Louisville
Slugger and held it with one hand, ready to make like
Mickey Mantle should the need arise.

"Don't come any closer!" he warned. His voice
echoed inside his mask.

One of the men neared. He pulled the scarf from his
face. Blood streamed from his nose and the corners of his

mouth. His teeth were brown and rotting. He grinned, and it was sickening. He couldn't have been anything more than a teenager.

"We have no problems with you," he said in a gravely voice. "We just want the girl."

"Step away," Guido said. He held the bat high above his head like a lumberjack.

"We said you can go, old man," growled another before lunging forward. Guido lashed out with the bat, barely missing. His old muscles screamed on the backswing. The kid danced back and chortled.

Something hit his leg from behind. It buckled as pain tore into his buttocks. He dropped to one knee. It took all his effort to grab Alyssa before he fell on her. He pulled her against his chest and swung the bat wildly. He felt the wooden shaft connect. Someone howled in pain.

"Asshole!" one of the kids yelled.

Guido held his ground. He rose on his pain-seared leg and twirled around, thrusting the bat forward as he did. He caught sight of the wounded assailant, hunched on the ground, holding his head. He coughed. The remaining four closed in, encircling them. He knew he couldn't hold them off forever. At his age, it was just a matter of time.

"Listen to me!" Guido shouted. "There was a radio broadcast! The French have arrived! They have ships waiting in Groton, and all we have to do is get there. You don't have to fight me on this!"

One of the attackers – still wearing his bloody scarf – swung his board. It missed, and that only seemed to make him angrier. "Fucking liar," he grunted.

"I'm not lying!" bellowed Guido. Alyssa's head buried further into his chest. He felt her body quiver as she sobbed. Regret filled him. That light, that hope, he'd seen earlier was gone. Anger shook him to the bone.

The one who'd spoken first piped up again, this time in a softer, calmer tone.

"Listen, man. No need to make shit up. We know we don't got long to go. Just let us have some fun before then, 'kay? C'mon, you're a man. You understand. Right?"

Guido couldn't believe the words. He struggled with Alyssa's weight, his breathing coarse and painful. "You won't get her," he whispered. He didn't think they could hear him beneath his mask. He didn't care.

With a sudden fury, Guido charged. The surprised kid didn't move fast enough. The bat struck his head, which snapped sideways, streaming blood like a morbid sprinkler. His body twisted and then lay still as it hit the ground

Alyssa's weight slowed Guido's movements as the others attacked with a vengeance. One hit him in the shoulder. He hunched, protecting his precious girl with his own body. Another struck his thigh. He fell over, the pain horrendous. He rolled as to not crush the Alyssa, and then huddled over her. Someone ripped his mask off. Gasping, he inhaled handfuls of wet ash and began to choke. Another blow, this one on his back. He felt the nail punch through his clothes and pierce his flesh. It drove in so deep that when it retreated it felt like it dragged his insides with it.

The world turned hazy. Everything shook.

Keep her safe, his reeling mind insisted. *Protect the girl, save the only one that matters.*

Blows landed all over his body. Rusty nails drove into him. He grew weaker and weaker by the second. Alyssa clung to him as he fell to the side. He felt his blood leak out through the numerous new holes in his body, soaking his clothes and dribbling down his chin. And still, the girl clutched him.

A savage hovered above, tugging on Alyssa's hand like a fairy-tale beast. The girl screamed and kicked, not letting go. He tried harder, and that made her kick all the more. Finally he reared back and lifted the board above his head. The nail glinted in the faint light. Guido pulled Alyssa below him and closed his eyes.

A shot cracked the air. Another. Then shouting. They surrounded him, a chorus of chaotic voices. Guido held the girl, wishing he had a womb into which he could stuff her for protection. He was about to die, and even worse, so was she. In the only thing he'd cared about in a long, long time, he'd failed.

But there were no more blows. The shouts ceased, as well as the gunshots. Guido lay still, afraid to move. Alyssa squirmed in his arms. He could hear her breathing inside her mask. It sounded like a freight train.

Hands grabbed his mangled body. They rolled him over. He felt weak, and with blurred vision he watched a man lift Alyssa up. He held her out as if inspecting a sensitive work of art. Beside him was another human form, this one was smaller and holding a rifle. It kicked the motionless body at its feet. Several others walked by, just ghosts in his foggy eyesight. Their voices chattered on.

A shadow blocked out his vision. A man's face. He wore a bandana over his nose and mouth, blood soaked like the others. The eyes though…blue, kind, and concerned.

"My name's Jason," the man said. "We're friendly. Who were those kids?"

"Gone wild," Guido said, his voice rough and weak. "And hungry…hungry for things they shouldn't, they shouldn't…"

Jason glanced over at Alyssa and then nodded to show he understood.

"She's all right now?" he asked, unable to look for himself.

"She is," Jason said. "She's with my daughter, Melissa."

Guido tried to nod, but didn't have the energy.

"Did you hear the announcement?" he heard a young girl ask, most likely Melissa.

Alyssa responded, still quivering but on the edge of excitement. "We did."

"They've come!" said the girl between coughs. "We'll be safe and warm!"

Guido felt a bit of gratitude as Jason lifted his head so he could see her better.

"We'll take care of her for you," he whispered. "What's her name?"

"Alyssa," Guido coughed. "My granddaughter."

Contented, he leaned his head back, smiled, and let the darkness take him.

Let It Continue
by David Dalglish

"Just a few more steps," John told his wife. "We're almost there."

Susan took his outstretched hand into her own.

"Thank God," she said, forcing a weary smile. "My feet feel ready to fall off."

John pulled her up the final flight of stairs to the third floor of what had once been an apartment complex in the northern stretches of Maine. The ash had fallen light there, so far to the east, and the building remained structurally sound. Rows of doors remained opened, broken by looters or left unlocked by former inhabitants as they'd fled. John couldn't imagine why they hadn't stayed. Of all the United States, Maine was the one state that had gone almost completely unscathed.

A bit of smoke trailed out from the second door to their right, and John led them just to the side. He let go of Susan's hand so he could grip his gun in both. His bullets were few, but he had enough to kill a man. He'd never been a good shot, not until the ash fell. Over the months since the ash fell, he'd learned quick.

"Hello?" John called, knocking on the wall beside the door. "My name's John Crawford, and I'm with my wife, Susan. We're looking for Faye."

He held his breath and listened for the telltale sounds of ammo clips and shotgun pumps. Nothing, only labored footsteps toward the door. He dared a glance around the corner.

"Julie send you?" a rail-thin black woman asked, her eyes large walnuts, her hair tied back in a ponytail. She stood in the center of the room, bundled in a multitude of coats and hats. In one corner was a pile of wood, broken and ready for burning. Where the stove used to be was a fire, its smoke billowing out a small hole in the roof. In the kitchen was a mini-fridge, its handle gray and smeared with dirt and ash.

"She did," John said, stepping full before the doorway. The woman's eyes flared at the sight of his gun, and with a subtle shift, she revealed a similar pistol clipped to her belt.

"I have no food to spare," the woman insisted. "Julie should have told you that. I help out when I can, but this ain't one of those…"

Faye stopped when Susan joined her husband's side. Her walnut eyes looked to Susan's swollen belly.

"Jesus," she said. "No wonder Julie sent you. Come on in, girl. The cold's no place for a pregnant woman."

"Thanks," Susan said. Because of her weight and the thick coats she wore, she waddled toward the small fire. Grunting with pleasure, she sat down before it and removed one of her coats.

"Benefits of being pregnant," Faye said as she hurried into her kitchen and started scrounging for food. "It's like having a little furnace in your belly. Keeps you nice and warm. Me, however…"

She laughed as she gestured to her thin frame, her eyes sunken into her face, her cheeks stretched, and her neck a thin piece of bone and veins.

"I take it you sleep close to the fire at night," John said, trying to make light of things.

"*In* the damn fire, and still not always warm," Faye said, laughing.

John sat beside his wife and removed two of his coats. The fire had a musty smell to it, but it was warm. He held his hands over it, closing his eyes and trying to relax. He clicked on the safety to his pistol as Faye sat a small plate of mixed vegetables from a can beside each of them.

"Heat it over the fire if you must," Faye said as she ate directly from the can with a spoon. "I've gotten used to it cold, though. Winter in Maine was never easy, but lately…I swear, it's like the ash blocked out the sun. What I'd give to be in South America right now, hell even Africa. Some days I think I'm hungry enough to wrestle a meal away from a lion."

She watched the couple eat while she sucked on the spoon.

"I know Julie sent you," she finally said. "But did she tell you *why* she was sending you my way?"

John removed his wife's second coat, pushed her long blond hair to the side of her neck, and then began massaging her shoulders.

"You're a nurse," he said.

"I was," Faye said. "Damn good one, too. Don't you have any worry, Mrs. Crawford. I've performed hundreds of these procedures, and I'll make sure nothing happens to you while I'm removing the fetus."

"Removing the…?" Susan pulled away from her husband.

"You said we were coming here for my labor," she said.

"I said we should be here before your labor starts," John said, but his words sounded like the words of a lawyer, not a husband.

"Is that what Julie said? That why she sent us here?"

"This is no world for a child," Faye said, her voice calm in the face of their anger. She'd seen a thousand arguments so very similar, and she knew how to let them roll over her without upsetting her. "You know this as well as I. There's no food, not for a baby."

"I'll have milk," said Susan.

"Milk ain't free," Faye said, shaking her head. "It's coming from you, and my old jackass of a boss wouldn't have been happy with how little weight you've gained during your pregnancy."

Susan stood. When she waivered unsteadily on her feet, John was there to help her. She pushed him away with a choked sob.

"Let go of me," she said. "I didn't carry this child for nine months just to give up."

She put on one of her coats and stormed out the door. John watched her go, a mixture of anger and helplessness on his face.

"She'll come around," he said, trying to force a smile. He did a poor job of it.

Faye shook her head and finished the last of her meal.

"Don't force her," she said. "You do, she'll hate you until she dies. I want you to remember something, John. I've done plenty of procedures, but I've helped deliver as well. I won't tell you what to do. You both have a decision to make. I won't say it's just hers, because she's got to rely on you for everything afterward in a world like this. Keep or not. Up to you. But if you do decide to keep it, you better be damn sure you know why."

John put on his coat and turned away.

"I'll keep that in mind," he said.

He went to his wife.

*

They slept beside the fire, doing their best to pretend Faye wasn't there. Susan lay curled into her husband's arms, his hands resting comfortable atop her breasts. His forehead pressed against her hair, and when he whispered, his breath warmed her ear.

"It wouldn't be right," he said.

"Like hell it wouldn't."

He kissed her neck.

"I don't want to," he said. "But what choice do we have? How many times have we nearly starved? Think of how bleak a future we'd give him. Or her. You remember the rapes? The riots?"

He quieted.

"I've forgiven you," she whispered.

"I haven't," he said. "Nine men, and one woman. That's how many I've killed to keep us together. To keep us alive. To bring a child into this godforsaken world would be cruel. Damn it all, there's sick fucks out there that would *eat* our baby if they had the chance."

She shivered in his arms, and he quieted when he realized she was crying. Feeling like an ass, he held her tight and kissed her neck.

"I'm sorry," he said.

For many long moments they lay silent, him grinding his teeth because he was upset and nervous, her sniffling and struggling to get her wild emotions under control. Susan had always considered herself a tough, logical woman. Being pregnant had taken that part of her and flung it into a blender, then pounded it with a thousand tons of ash.

"Is that what you really want?" she asked.

He bit down his initial response and gave it a moment of honest thought.

"No," he finally said. "I don't. But I'm scared to death of what could happen to our child. I don't see any reason for hope. None. How do I give life up to that?"

"But I can feel it move," she whispered. "You have, too. You've felt it kick."

This time it was his turn to fight the sniffles.

"I hate this," he said. "I fucking hate this."

It took several hours before they fell asleep, light and restless and without dreams.

*

When John awoke, his wife was gone. He bolted to his feet, staggering about the room collecting his coat and hat. Faye stirred, then covered her face as a slice of light met her eye from him opening the door.

"Where are you going?" she asked.

"Susan," he said, as if that explained everything.

"She's probably out taking a piss," Faye said.

John shook his head and left the warmth for the frozen outside. He had a feeling in his gut, too strong to ignore. Something was wrong. Susan had left him, but why? As he climbed down the stairs, he shook his head. No, that was a dumb question to ask himself. He knew why. Of course he knew why. The better question now was where?

Out from the cover of the building he felt the first touches of a snow falling lightly against his cheek. The touch immediately sent shivers up his shoulders and across his neck. He hated snow, had for months now. It reminded him too much of that first blizzard of ash. They'd piled into their car, just him and Susan, and fled their Kentucky home. He thought of all the horrors he'd seen, driven through, even driver *over*...

"Susan?" he called out, trying to break himself free of his own thoughts. "Susan, where are you babe?"

The apartment complex had been built on the edge of town, and stretching out across it was a long field, fenced in with barbed wire. The snow was light, but he could see feint depressions that might have been footsteps. Pulling his gloves tighter against his fingers, he ducked underneath and followed. The further he followed her into the field, the more certain he became of her passing. Worse, though, was how he also saw the field stretching on and on for seemingly endless miles, yet no sign of his wife.

Suddenly this was no temper tantrum, no whim of a pregnant lady enslaved to her hormones. This wasn't a marital spat. The wind was biting, the snow gradually thickening in ferocity. Feeling a moment of panic, he looked back to ensure the apartment remained, still visible in the white. Snow and ash had buried half the world, but at least Faye and her warm shelter were still there, still standing. He almost thought he could see the yellow glow of a fire.

"Susan!" he shouted. "Where are you?"

He trudged on, following the footprints. At first he thought he might lose sight of them completely, but then Susan must have reached a place of thicker snow, the depressions too thick to be buried just yet. John's pace quickened, first to a brisk pace, then a jog. His breath burst out of him in white wisps of frost. He quit yelling. His mind was too occupied with horrific images of his wife lying in the snow, her limbs frozen, her eyes waxy and unblinking.

And then he did find her, hidden behind a small drift built up against a row of bushes. She sat with her legs to her chest, her face pressed against her knees. To John's horror, she'd cast off both her coats.

"Please, no, go away," she sobbed as he flung his arms around her. She shrieked and flailed against his touch, and so shocked was he that when her fingernails drew blood from his cheek, he didn't even feel it.

"Susan, babe…what's wrong. What's going…"

Her coats were already covered in snow, their heat long gone. Braving her fury, he opened his own coats and tried to envelop her again. Her face was a frightening shade of gray, her lips quivering and blue. She moved to fight him, but he only shushed her with a kiss against her forehead. She broke down sobbing in his arms, curling into him to share his warmth.

As she cried, he surveyed the area. He could think of only one reason she'd come out into the middle of nowhere and cast off both her coats. Just one reason. And it scared him more than he'd ever been since that first storm of ash.

"Why?" he asked once her sobs had settled down to sniffles. "Why'd you do this? How could you?"

"Because you're right," she said through chattering teeth. "You're right, but I can't do it. You'd convince me. You always do. But I'd rather die than lose our child. Either way, our baby's dead. At least she'd die in me. She'd die warm and whole, and I wouldn't have to try sleeping at night thinking of…thinking of…"

And then she was crying again. John felt tears trying to build in his own eyes, but the sharp wind stole them away.

"Never," he said. "I could never live without you. You're all I have. Can't you see that? You're why I've survived since this whole shitstorm started."

He chuckled, forced and bitter.

"You can't imagine how many horrible thoughts went through my head. What I was worried I might find. If you were…you know…I think I'd have laid down right there next to you. All I've got is my love for you, and no matter what, I can't let go of that."

He kissed her forehead and sniffed. She looked up at him, her eyes red and puffy.

"And that's what I feel for our baby. That's what I was doing. You love me? Then let it continue. Let it grow."

They stood, her wrapping an arm around his waist as he kept his coats tight about her. Together they made the march back toward the complex even as the snow and wind and cold did its best to slow them.

They stepped into the apartment room, Susan still pale from the chill. Faye stirred from her rest beside the fire.

"She all right?" Faye asked.

John nodded.

"Faye," he said. "We have our decision."

"And what is that?"

Susan clutched her husband as if afraid she'd lose him.

"It has to continue," she said. "Life. Love. It can't stop. It's all we have. It's all we've ever had."

Faye ran a hand through her hair.

"You're sure?" she asked.

They nodded, both of them. Faye smiled.

"All right, then," she said. "We'll let it continue."

Note from the Author:

Anyone who has read anything by me knows this collection is a rather large departure from what I normally write. Usually I'm in a world of elves, orcs, and magic. Yet with Land of Ash, I wanted to test myself, see if I could honestly write beyond my comfort zone. I'd recently read much of Ray Bradbury, and there was a story in there in which the whole world is told in their dreams that life would end that night, yet no one rioted. No one panicked. It was hopeful, calm, and beautiful. With such ideals in mind, I wrote what became the first story, One Last Dinner Party.

OLDP enjoyed a bit of popularity in a fellow indie author's collection, The Lake and 17 Other Stories, so much so that I wanted to see if I could delve deeper into this potential devastation. Borrowing from Bradbury yet again, I went for a Martian Chronicles feel, with various characters, places, and times instead of a single narrative. Might as well follow what you know works, eh?

I should probably mention the whole science aspect of this. By no means am I pretending to be an authority figure on the Yellowstone Caldera's eruption. I had little to go on, and much of it from the internet (and we know how trusty that is, right?). Everyone agrees the eruption would be catastrophic, but just how and in what ways is a bit iffy. I went with what would let me write the best stories. Story trumps science, at least for me. I hope I kept things realistic, but let's be honest here, this collection isn't about the ash. It's about the characters, their choices, their trials, as they try to endure a fate that would shock many to their core.

I hope you enjoyed yourself. I want to say thanks to Ron Hearn, for the inspiration for this whole eruption.

Thanks also to David, Daniel, John, Rob, and Mike for working with me to add some new voices to this collection. Fingers crossed that you had fun reading their contributions as well.

Again, thank you. Your time is precious, dear reader, and I'm glad you spent it with me.

David Dalglish
November 5, 2010

A little bit about my friends…

David McAfee is the author of the horror novels 33 A.D., GRUBS, and SAYING GOODBYE TO THE SUN. He has also published two short story collections: THE LAKE AND 17 OTHER STORIES and A POUND OF FLASH. He and his wife currently live in Knoxville, TN, where they are awaiting the birth of their first child.

Daniel Arenson is an author of fantasy fiction, from epic to dark and surreal. He's written dozens of stories and poems, and is the author of fantasy novels Firefly Island (2007), Flaming Dove (2010), and The Gods of Dream (forthcoming). Visit Daniel's website at DanielArenson.com

John Fitch V is the author of several fantasy and sci-fi novels, including The Obloeron Trilogy, One Hero A Savior, the baseball time travel epic Turning Back The Clock and A Galaxy At War. Find out more at www.johnfitchv.com.

Michael Crane is the author of IN DECLINE and LESSONS AND OTHER MORBID DRABBLES. He is a graduate of Columbia College Chicago with a BA in Fiction Writing. Michael currently lives in Illinois.

Robert J. Duperre lives in northern Connecticut with his wife, the artist Jessica Torrant, his three wonderful children, and Leonardo the one-eyed wonder yellow Lab. He is the author of the Rift Series, a demon and zombie apocalypse. You can read more about Robert and his views and ideas by visiting robertduperre.com.

Made in the USA
Lexington, KY
08 July 2012